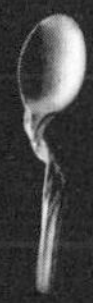

A PRAGUE FLÂNEUR

PHOTO : V. NEZVAL

. . . and at a loss for what to do at this hour of insipid light, this afternoon hour so perfectly expressed by a solitary, bare boat . . . p. 11

Vítězslav Nezval

A PRAGUE FLÂNEUR

Translated from the Czech by Jed Slast

Photographs by the author

TWISTED SPOON PRESS

PRAGUE

2024

ISBN: 978-80-88628-00-2 (softcover)
ISBN: 978-80-88628-31-6 (e-book)

CONTENTS

JUNE 1937 – JULY 1938

Even when the composition of a book is preordained, as with *A Prague Flâneur*, everything still depends on how the present moment opens its gates.

On the day of June 9, 1937, after visiting the publishing house to whom most of my work has been entrusted, having relocated to the Topič Building, to hand in the manuscript of *The Absolute Gravedigger*, and at a loss for what to do at this hour of insipid light, this afternoon hour so perfectly expressed by a solitary, bare boat floating past, I headed toward Smíchov to see a friend who was in the process of moving and to lend him a hand with boxing up his books — and after a glance at his helpers finishing up their work convinced me that my assistance would clearly serve no purpose, I was momentarily astonished that my steps were unwittingly taking me to the Kinský Garden.

A long time has passed since I last sat — and alone at that — in this park, which will always signify spring for me, the springs of 1920 and 1921. In my mind's eye I saw Jiří Wolker as he appeared then, sitting on a bench in front of the

Empire-style museum, and before I sat down myself and pulled from my pocket the prospectus given to me at the publisher's just a short while before, the following inscription appeared on the bench before my astounded eyes:

Wolker and Nezval

During those years when ration tickets were still required to buy cigarettes, this was the park where new music enthralled me for the first time, where I would be reborn into a new sensibility. Evenings on Mělnická Street, giddy mornings and mad birds at dawn when returning from nocturnal trysts, Wolker's Café Finále, the charcuterie with its alluring student treats, the wickerwork bakery, and the crazy professor in the brown bowler — an incomplete, yet for me utterly exhilarating inventory of those years.

It's been a long time since I've sat in the park, and being here allowed me to return to my former sensibilities. I have always associated this park with a certain chateau garden where I once met the poet Jakub Deml, his house near to where friends were living. This was later on, and it was dismal because you had to sit there in the morning or in the evening during the days leading up to summer vacation, as if sitting in a park of freedom prior to graduation, for the women with braids to be different, so they would be new. I have never been inside the museum — what a quaint little chateau! Yes, you had to sit there like a student and jot down your thoughts in a notebook on bent knees, to compose a nocturne, an improvisation on piano, each moment presenting an opportunity to speak to the woman sitting on the neighboring bench — and then find yourself conversing with her.

The park closes at eight p.m., and the birds, they actually do exist. As do the couples. As does the person who sits there as if on the cusp of graduating from gymnasium.

You realize what it means to be a "flâneur" as soon as you're fated to be chairbound. The antithesis of a throne, this chair is a cobbler's stool, for working — and life is fleeting.

Maybe this is why the role of the "flâneur" seems so ideal, because life is indeed fleeting. When we walk — and especially when we walk with no destination in mind — the faint images of our desire impose themselves on our steps and prevents us from seeing its end, its converse.

The wait for something to ignite in me the expectation of a moment of joy, along with the rain keeping me inside, compels me to roam from book to book.

The baffling news that keeps appearing about the execution of eight Soviet generals — and this incessant rain, so much like the rain in Moscow, has fated me today, in self-torment, to open only certain books and not others.

In Trotsky's *The History of the Russian Revolution* I search for a clue to what is currently playing out in the East; in a printed edition of one of Bukharin's lectures, which I heard him deliver in person, I search for some clue to what later landed him in prison. And reading his speech, inarguably such a constructive contribution in 1934, my heart is heavy, made so by the surfeit of abstract thinking, which at one time seemed to be unavoidable as soon as the talk turned to poetry, made so by the absolute incomprehension of the miraculous essence of poetry that is able to gloss the “simplicity” of Demyan Bedny with these words: “But this is not the studied, artificial primitiveness affected by the refined and spiritless representatives of a tired culture, which, from wearisome complexity and the pretentiousness of hypertrophied artificiality, is attracted to a caricature-like reproduction of bushmen drawings, Negro dances, etc., reminding one of the idiotic lisping of grown-ups in the presence of infants.”

And I am saddened to think of all those Marxist aestheticians who, inundated by proofs both dialectical and anti-dialectical, both pro and con, have entirely forgotten about the child in us, the child in socialism.

At this point — and not too long ago I would have thought this virtually impossible — the simple, purely elemental, concrete, authentic figure of Stalin rises up before me as a savior resolutely applying the brakes to all this problematic, speculative abstraction, as a directive to reality, as a directive to restraint. This man, who bends down to the faces of children, embraces the bellicose, and is said to prefer reading Shakespeare over RAPP writers, this man seems closer to my heart particularly now (how odd!) when so many heads are falling, when so many heads had to fall.

And I cannot help but think of Lautréamont’s *Poésies* and the requisites for good delivered by a man (by this very man) who in pain avenged himself on every evil by flinging it without a whit of caution in the faces of all in the cantos of *Les Chants de Maldoror*.

The hour has passed when poets will sing in delight over rivers of blood. Its most terrible eddy flowing right past our eyes might finally convince the poets of Revolution, the poets with hope for a more just tomorrow, that it is incumbent to bury the world of sophists and over their bloody shades greet the red dawn of beneficence glowing in a small building of the great Kremlin.

As I walk through Prague's streets on days when airplanes frantically vie with one another in the June sky, the thought that these streets, these towers and walls, these roofs that are here now might all at once cease to exist, awakens in my heart a great compassion, a great love and hope that thanks to the deluge of blood in the land of long rains sophistry has now run its course. And I greet differently than before this city and the Stalin Constitution of peace, a peace we all so desire, a peace so desired for a country that has made this dialectical leap, the consequence of which is everything, absolutely everything, happening around us.

If this leap could be stayed at its height, it might be enough to automatically cause the demise of all these hideous regimes preparing for war.

And maybe the Prague flâneur's love for the city that is his fate and the fate of his nation, maybe this love, piqued by danger, will be outlived by the roofs, streets, and shopwindows his involuntary meditation has presently supplanted.

The weather cleared on the evening of June 15, 1937, and this allowed me to interrupt my musings and go out.

I would've liked to attend a performance that day of Guillaume Apollinaire's *The Breasts of Tiresias*, which fifteen years earlier was so important for all of us, for the entire milieu in which we lived then. Encountering this play epitomized for me those avant-garde gatherings still fresh in my mind today. Yes, at that time (it was at Café Hlavova — God knows how we ended up there, but we alternated between many cafés then — Hanau Pavilion, Žofín Palace, the Municipal Commons, the Municipal House, to name some of the occasional venues for our meetings) our conversation was peppered with passages from Apollinaire's Surrealist drama and someone remarked that it was necessary "to do everything that can be done with imagination."

See the Hanau Pavilion, where we go to annihilate the tedium of a Sunday; see Žofín Palace at the time of the picture poem, which conceptually is not entirely unlike the "poem-object" that emerged around 1935, a time when I was preoccupied with the idea of constructing an automaton that would produce poetry for all five senses; see the Municipal House, whose café we visit on the day *Život* appears to throw a scare into the traditional artists, the café where the Siren was sitting, where on a magnificent early summer day Poetism was born; see the Municipal Commons, where we gather to remember Wolker, who was fading from our thoughts.

How glad I was now to greet my young friends in front of the theater on Na Zbořenci where they were performing *The Breasts of Tiresias*.

Such fond memories. Those boys brought me back to the electric atmosphere in the small Na Slupi theater when I participated in afternoon rehearsals, reading with Jarmila Horáková the parts from *Dispatch on Wheels*, when I glanced through the doorway at a passing funeral, when I picked up the card for good luck lying near me on the ground, when I played a flexatone during a performance of Aristophanes's *Women at the Thesmorphia*, when I leaned over the stairwell or attended my evening premiere.

Alas, a chance encounter now prevented me from going in. I walked the streets only for the pleasure of walking.

I ran into Josef Čapek near the Topič Bookstore, and this meeting was all the more endearing to me in that several of my afternoon meditations had spontaneously elicited a contrast with his reflections in *The Gimpy Pilgrim*, which I only now realized. Josef Čapek was holding a cane.

When he graciously complimented my matching white coat and white hat, he began to relate an anecdote that ineluctably brought to my mind one of his illustrations for Apollinaire's *The Heresiarch & Co.* He told me that one time at the end of Legion Bridge he met a writer who had long fallen silent, and indeed from time to time I as well would see his hunchback figure tottering along by the National Theater. Well, at one moment the man was standing at the Malá Strana end of the bridge, tapping with his little cane, and a short moment later, unobserved by Čapek, who was walking across the bridge toward the National Theater, he was spotted in the same stance now at the other end of the bridge, opposite the National Theater. And this phantom reappeared twice more in short succession, now at the end of National Avenue, now at the end of Na Příkopě Street.

The comical explanation for these ghostly occurrences (the writer had recently purchased a monthly tram pass and entertained himself by getting off at each stop and waiting for the next tram to come along), did not detract from how marvelous I found the story, and the fact that it had been told by the author of *The Gimpy Pilgrim* doubly reinforced my vision of a Prague flâneur.

Be that as it may, it was Apollinaire who put Prague in the title of his story and — I do not hesitate to say — he was one of the first responsible for awakening in me what he called a "new sensibility."

I consider poetry to be nothing other than this "new sensibility." As soon as this "new sensibility" took hold in me, everything took on a different meaning. And it seems to me that the most fateful misunderstandings between critics and creators is over this very point. Nothing determines all the poet's steps to such a degree as does a "new sensibility," and no problems, no matter how intractable or pressing will ever alter this fact.

It was this "new sensibility" that allowed me to experience Moscow and Paris in the way I did and not in any other way. And this "new sensibility" guides my steps through Prague today, even at this very moment.

I accompanied Josef Čapek across Legion Bridge and felt the encounter had given this book special validation.

The pilgrim and the flâneur, these two approximate expressions coined for one and the same activity, gave me above all a palpable sense of their difference. It was not my lot to savor the joy of meditation. And the hunchbacked walker being miraculously conveyed from one place to the next was Josef Čapek's profound understanding for my condition.

I unexpectedly found myself among the streets of Vinohrady when visiting a friend on June 19.

I had been drinking heavily the night before and slept little. My delight from the sudden cascade of this walk was

JOSEF ČAPEK

. . . an anecdote that ineluctably brought to my mind one of his illustrations for Apollinaire's *The Heresiarch & Co.* p. 17

somewhat muted. I had no taste for cigarettes. And yet, this sullen mood presented to me a Vinohrady suddenly bathed in the light of discovery, in the form I knew it by best.

And this is why I had long abhorred it! It was the cause of my misery as a student, which on top of the steady degradation of self-esteem and penury, almost always my own fault, was perpetuated by the wretchedness of my rented lodgings. How alien it was! Alien furniture, apathetic curtains, nothing I would have chosen myself, nothing that would have reflected in any way my desire. Alien steps beyond the wall, alien voices, alien laughter. This alienness came to fill everything, this entire neighborhood, and it cleaved to my loves.

The Vinohrady charcuteries where one and the same flavor topped all the others. And the alien streetwalkers, the alien university environment, the terrible alienness that prevented only myself from hearing the less vibrant trumpeting of this quarter. The awful landlords, watching your every step, your loves, your comings and goings, your entire vapid life!

I moved to Sokolská Street. It was here that I was treated to a little hotel freedom — and it was here that love was drawn from the murky well into the light of day. It meant the world to me. And although it entailed abject poverty, although I had to sacrifice a number of beautiful books to an antiquarian, books I will never get back, although I lived on milk, I was free, I was a poet, nothing was shackling my sovereign gift — freedom.

Much has been written ad nauseam about freedom, and its limits have rightly been drawn. And yet — its luminous essence is the freedom of desire. This is what I learned on Sokolská Street, this is what I won there, as if by chance.

Having given notice of vacating the room where I had spent a year of my life — which I had written mechanically, without any serious thought, as if it were part of a game — I brought my papers and books to my hotel room, where I was free, where I was happy. Several random circumstances conspired to keep me from dying of hunger. But I was free.

The melancholy of my steps now immersed me in the former atmosphere of those desperate days, though Vinohrady itself was scintillating. It sparkled like the beautiful daughters of parvenus, those beautiful pampered daughters, whose bracelets shall be discounted so that all women might be beautiful.

I could employ those old feelings of being unfree to conjure up images of heinous social bondage, for which the moneybags of this district are to blame. I could put myself in the shoes of all the wretched victims of this unjust social order and thoroughly depress you. Yes, the dispiriting, anti-poetic side of proletarian and socially conscious poetry comes from the very fact that such poets have been so pleased to depress us. This I will not do. My philosophy, which is at one with the philosophy of the revolutionary working class, is one of hope.

I was despondent and liberated myself from this gloom, but alas it was only an individual matter. Even then my despondency came from a sleepless night, and I awakened from it. I know that all, yes, all will awaken from their sleepless social night, of this I am certain. And I shall never consent to contribute to a universal dejection.

Evening is approaching. I am sitting on the back terrace of Mánes and the sun is setting behind Petřín Hill.

Soon Prague will be teeming with terraces. In the afternoon as I was deciding which one of several I should visit in the heart of the city (sadly, too few!), my quest couldn't help but spur in me the memory of one café terrace located in Moscow during the time of the All-Union Congress of Soviet Writers. It was the terrace of the Red Poppy.

It was truly wonderful to sit there among people who had already made the revolutionary leap. The hope inspired, truly uplifting! Now, as the reddening sky between the hills of Petřín and Hradčany, the reddening sky on the Vltava to which I turn my eyes, brings to an end one magnificent summer day, the sight of swallows circling the tower of the former mill fills me with anxiety.

And before I could register that I saw them as airplanes, one of them sliced across the Petřín tower and disappeared under the wireless telegraphy pylon only to remerge beyond the hill, flying off in the direction of Hřebenka.

If I had opened a newspaper, I would have seen so much ink devoted to the imminence of war. The threat of war, the threat to destroy all these café terraces, this Petřín Hill, these castle towers. The threat to destroy this city through which I walk. And maybe this is the very danger that must be averted, no matter what the cost, and to do this the Soviet Union will sacrifice all its days and its good name; maybe this is the very danger that for two years, two springs and two summers, has caused me to observe how a "new sensibility" toward Prague has been awakening inside me.

Having little to do with pathos, this "new sensibility"

impels me to pause before Prague as if it were a violin, as if testing the tuning by quietly plucking at its strings, no matter what kind they might be. This "new sensibility," lacking articulation and historical context, has turned me into a tuner who converts everything he meets into a single tone, into the tone of an emotion without sentimentality, without pathos, without meditation.

This "new sensibility," which materializes in split-second encounters, no matter where, which does not distinguish beauty by the categories of important or unimportant, which wanders under the open sky and is at the center of life itself, this "new sensibility," without pretense, without ethics, without aesthetics, and without utility, has made me a Prague flâneur.

On June 21, the absence of one of those whom I visit now and again to request an advance on a finished work that would enable me to live for a while carefree (not long of course!), that is, without a thought of what will happen tomorrow or the next day (this is how I live now, how I've been accustomed to living for years) presented me with two hours of nothing to do — and since it was one of those mild summer days for which I like to throw myself into the blaze of a responsive trance, my steps chose a circuitous route that I've taken with some regularity over the past three years, my delight still undiminished, as if on this roundabout way I might meet with an unforeseen adventure, an unforeseen stroke of luck.

I enjoy the inanity of lingering before shopwindows with

displays of lingerie, ties, stationery items, and those marvelous tobacco products.

After all, there are more of these types of shops between National Avenue and the end of Na Příkopě than anywhere else in Prague, and here their allure is even greater since nearly everything in them is beyond my means.

Undoubtedly these beautiful ties, which I would love to alternate according to the sun, these delightful shirts, which envelop us with just a hint of femininity, these ingenious products, which, of course, I shall not purloin and which are like the most tender letters from the dearest friends (letters awaited daily with admirable patience), have their wellspring in our little irrational pleasures, our little emotional adventures, which are not devoid of poetry.

A reddish tie bearing the subtle images of embryos that will only ever beget brief delight and long pain, a yellowish or grayish shirt that creates the illusion that love is in the offing, or a pipe with either the straight or curved profile of an ideal woman, they will always inhabit our solitude with an evanescent happiness in which our desire is fulfilled obliquely and symbolically.

You, reader, who might consider my reflections indecorous (yes, I too feel how little we have shared in the consumption of the wealthy's lovely tinsel — and I am well aware of how many have no prospect of a small advance to wrest them for several days from the grips of . . . but enough!), and so suspect me of social insensitivity, I can only affirm that my European eyes witnessed in the most concrete, most intelligible way the nascent new Soviet optimism before the shopwindows on Moscow's Petrovka Street — and the appearance of this optimism in the eyes of Soviet men and women, in this concrete form, as they gazed at the miraculous multiplication of those dear objects, was not affected ("we produced it, we own it!"), but uncommonly ingenuous, even tender ("it's beautiful, I want it, but I'll get it tomorrow, or the day after, or when . . ."), uncommonly sybaritic.

My antipathy to capitalists does not come from the belief that they have everything, that they have more than everything, that they have, could have, it all (with or without joy, but that's irrelevant), but from the belief that their "have" implies "not have" for the majority of humanity — and the animus I feel will never devolve into the glamor they possess, whether great or small, and which we do not, cannot, possess.

As my eyes turn away from the empty, fraudulent, supercilious, or benign, though almost always heartless, soulless faces of the men and women who wear those beguiling meretricious trinkets, for which I confess a weakness, my absolute attention is directed at what shrouds the pedestrians on Na Příkopě Street.

Yes, I do like those magnificent bottles with even more magnificent labels, while I despise the poison that is spellbound inside, contained, that spills out of them.

From there I like to walk down Celetná Street, down that thoroughfare where I can already sense that most characteristic Prague skyline.

No matter how fashionable, no item, no book, even if it came out this very week, could ever alter the old-world ambience of the Hynek Bookshop in whose storerooms I would like to discover one day those penny dreadfuls that so enchanted my nannies.

No matter how modern, no amenity could ever deprive the Peterson Pipe Shop of its archaic gloom, much like the single-track electric tram line that replaced the rather poor horsecars of before, and no matter how new, no apartment house could ever alter the channel that is Celetná Street, nor divert its course away from the marvel of Old Town Square.

In the spring of 1935, André Breton, Paul Eluard, and I went into one of the oldest Prague wine bars so that I could be stunned (it was afternoon) by the ground-floor window situated under a high vaulted ceiling in which stood, magnificent as ever, the astronomical clock on Old Town Hall.

There is no greater pleasure than to have your perspective shifted so as to see something beloved in a new way.

And how supremely beautiful it was that on June 28, 1937, I could see the Vltava and its bridges, the Smíchov riverfront from a vantage that would not have existed if the back area of Mánes had not been turned into the summer terrace we named "Florida."

When standing on the embankment, the view of the Vltava appears provisional. This is because we look at it as we walk. And the standstill we are brought to by such an astonishing view is just our more leisurely tempo.

It has been nearly a year since one of those creatures, from whom every now and again something might be expected, we know not what, just something they've yet to offer, asked me if I had noticed anything unusual in the air the previous evening that had lent Prague a new splendor.

Although I wasn't sure what she had in mind, I did find

that particular evening so singularly stirring that I was at a complete loss for how to explain it. And yet as my girlfriend said, it was in the air — as if palpable. She said she read in the newspaper that a rare meteorological event had in fact occurred the previous evening. I regret to say that I only experience such unexpected meteorological phenomena before a single word. And that word is love.

Maybe this time, too, it was nothing more than just objective atmospheric fluctuations reinforced by natural conditions (the nearness of water, or vapors I couldn't detect) that produced a similar effect to the left bank of the Vltava with its houses and turrets, the dark passageways under the bridges, and even the sky, being exactly the same as the ones I've long admired in the paintings of Antonín Slavíček.

If I'm allowed a brief digression, I recall it was one summer evening several years ago, completely enveloped in a sudden downpour, that the unimaginable sheen of the streets and umbrellas opened to me, at the side of my beloved, the secret gate to the marvelous realm of this Impressionist.

But dusk was quickly descending, and the light that gave this evening its power and became a brush refashioning the Vltava's left bank into that painter's world (I love such validation through art) was fading into the violet depths, now wholly night.

And the red signal on the railroad bridge in the distance along which trundle illumined tram cars was a signal to me that I should return to the start of my circuitous route, although at the moment my spirit was centered on something other than the charm of these footsteps, which I didn't understand anyway.

Appearing before me was the most vivid moment of my former enthusiasm when, still a stranger in Prague, feeling low more often than not, I walked full of trepidation across Legion Bridge and imbibed the mystery that for me pervaded the ever tremulous and wondrously vertical lights reflecting off the Vltava's surface.

These enigmatic lights were the first mesmerizing eyes that Prague cast on me. And if, apart from them, I was drawn almost exclusively to other such lights (equally mysterious amid the darkness of obscure alleyways), lights such as that of the nightclub *Le Chat noir*, it was doubtless because behind these and behind them, invisible and yet present, present through her mesmerizing eyes, hid a singing Siren.

From the moment this book took on life (ah, how much longer will it hold me in its sway), I have had the feeling that when I walk through Prague I am seeking a collaborator in the marvelous, male or female, who would help me externalize the light I see, the light that so dazzles me.

On June 25, I was walking around Prague with a young man who was soon to make his debut as a poet when all of a sudden, right by the tram stop on National Avenue, a golden head flashed by, the name of its bearer slipping from my companion's lips and inadvertently directing our steps toward the show window of the Rubeš Gallery, to where she had suddenly started to run, so suddenly that my friend feared she was running away from him.

Barely a month later, likewise in the company of this same man and in a similar frame of mind as now, I encountered

ANTONÍN SLAVÍČEK

. . . I love such validation through art . . . p. 27

this woman, and very little stood in the way of our being introduced.

On another day he had told me in passing that she was interested in trying her luck in the theater.

Now as I approached her from three steps away I could not contain my astonishment that between the day we should have been introduced on National Avenue and this afternoon a delightful little incident had occurred whose heroine was none other than this golden-haired woman.

It was just ten days earlier when, in the company of one of those elegant ladies with whom I enjoy strolling through more unfamiliar places, I found myself stupefied on the Petřín Terrace, to where we had returned after a short downpour, by the rather unusual and adorable movements of a young blonde who quite abruptly had gotten up from the table of a young fellow with whom she had been engaged in intimate conversation, came over to our table, and with a terse apology bent down to pick up from the floor a rose she said had fallen under the table here and belonged to her.

My lady friend and I were enchanted. It was sweet, it was bold and gentle, very much in the nature of a young girl.

How did I not recognize her! Ah, in truth I felt I did know her, but from where? I couldn't recall. If I'm not mistaken, I likely associated her with one of the cafés I frequented, with Mánes, or with a students' carnival.

Now when I recollected the little incident with the rose and apologized for not having recognized her then, I couldn't express my feelings any other way than by caressing her shoulder and gazing into her eyes.

As for my friend, who knew her a little and was happy we

had the chance to meet, he displayed so much exuberance the story about the rose was soon forgotten and our mood became pleasantly buoyant, with my friend and the girl sardonically commenting on student life and its privations.

As for her, she confessed to being in a hurry to get to Smíchov. She needed to go somewhere near the train station to pick up payment for private lessons given to someone who, she said, would likely cancel the next day's lesson. Why shouldn't we accompany her when I had very little hope of finding in one of these random shops the piano sheet music for *The Threepenny Opera*, which had been my mission at that moment?

I will not describe our route along the riverbank, across Jirásek Bridge, and then along the main avenue in Smíchov as the lovely prattle of my two companions was not intended to inspire deeper impressions. As my mind persistently returned to that inauspicious piano music, I could hear the girl's mouth emitting a few bars of this or that song from *The Threepenny Opera* and was astonished to learn that she was a student at the conservatory and was currently writing an exhaustive study on a rather eccentric, abrasive, virtually forgotten genius.

I was confused how to reconcile so many contradictory impressions, all the more since between the time the girl left us to go collect her fee and when she returned I learned some baffling information that suggested this cheerful, pert, somewhat sheepish creature had been through hard times.

On the way through Smíchov, I occasionally took her hand tenderly and smiled at her. Apart from these trifling attentions, which I found oddly stimulating, I was utterly distracted, silent, hardly saying a word the whole time.

Now near Přemyslová Street the recollection of a magnificent butterfly encased in a globe led me to ask my friend and the girl if they would kindly accompany me to check if this globe, which had so delighted André Breton that I unsuccessfully tried to acquire it from the obstinate lady who owned the ironing shop in whose window it sparkled, was still there.

I saw it from a distance, just as resplendent as it had appeared to me two years earlier.

Its owner still would not budge, continuing to insist that under no circumstances would she part with this small gift from one of the girls who worked for her. She remembered me, as well as the "French guy with the pouf," but all my pleading fell on deaf ears.

The girl found the lady's affection for her keepsake touching, and I was swathed in a veneer of heartache that I would not be bringing some joy to André Breton and his wife, Jacqueline Lamba, who had been crestfallen that this small object was unobtainable, an object more dear to me now after having not too long ago deciphered, or so it seemed to me, the irrational meaning it could have had for Breton and his wife.

Was this butterfly in a globe not a spontaneous foreshadowing of the daughter who was to come into the world and be given the name of Aube, who had already begun her invisible life inside Jacqueline at the time this globe had so powerfully captivated her?

Now this coincidence was associated with a special surprise for me, accentuated by the fact that the hair of the girl in our company was virtually the same color as the hair of the woman who commanded my boundless respect.

Just as we arrived at the Smíchov end of Legion Bridge, my friend handed the golden-haired girl a nosegay of red poppies from a flower seller, and in wild enthusiasm I added a bunch of mixed summer wildflowers and experienced the joy of seeing the proud look of the girl who suddenly had an armful of flowers.

When I leaned over the bridge above the Vltava into which my friend had just tossed a coin, I caught myself making a gesture that infallibly convinced me of my desire for the girl with the flowers, and I was abundantly aware that this gesture did not, could not, escape her notice.

She now spoke little, and she wanted to keep off the main streets as well. When we found ourselves on Ovocný trh, the open former fruit market area, I could not resist the temptation to give her another bouquet.

As the three of us dined together in a hotel cafeteria, I repeated my impulsive gesture, and when my friend left, remarking he would be gone for only a few minutes, I looked into the eyes of this extraordinary woman, who for a second time had set me on the path of chance, and we kissed.

Accompanying her steps initiated by this kiss not only bemused me, recoloring the streets of Vinohrady into a magical city, but gave me the hope that I would see her tomorrow at the place of her own choosing, on Petřín Hill, at that same table where her rose had nearly been trampled.

How enraptured I was, how bewildered! It seemed to me this was the guide the Prague flâneur had been anticipating from a miracle, embodying in human form all the magical signs of love that would overcome me unawares at shopwindows.

I felt as if I were kissing Prague with an old and yet new, entirely new kiss in the most erogenous spots.

Then it happened that a day later I was standing at the side of my girlfriend in the Seminary Garden. I'd never walked through this garden, and was excited that it resembled those old country gardens from my childhood.

This little comment of mine and the few kisses we dared to leave behind among the trees awakened in the woman with the rose a series of reminiscences that told me something about her life. I was beyond elated when she linked her arm in mine and continued to assure me how good she felt, how happy she was.

When we left the garden out to Újezd Street, as I walked beside her practically in an embrace, a miracle put in our way two small, barely thirteen-year-old girls. One looked at me intently and said my name. It was as absurd as it was beautiful.

Unfortunately, the woman with whom I felt so good had to leave in an hour to where my eyes could not accompany her, where my eyes could no longer give her their attentions. We got into a taxi, and as it transported us up to a summer restaurant at Pohořelec, our lips would not be denied their kisses, their blandishments.

Two days later I had the pleasure to sit with her for a few quickly passing hours on that terrace overlooking the Vltava and allow myself to be transported by her peculiar affections, her peculiar game, her purity, audacity, tenderness. There had been those who had tried to poison her *joie de vivre*. She was sorry that today as well she wouldn't be able to stay with me; she was sad, so she said, since at the place she would rather

PHOTO : V. NEZVAL

Now near Přemyslová Street the recollection of a magnificent butterfly encased in a globe . . . p. 32

not return to she couldn't confess what had kept her, confess why she was happy, so unbelievably happy. She told me this happiness had suffused everything she was going through and would go through.

For three days she'd known I would be leaving the next day, and she asked me to stay, at least another week so that we could see each other when she got back from the countryside.

We attracted attention. Oh, how were we any different than any other couple sitting here? She had to go — and happy I would accompany her. We took a taxi. I felt a word on her lips, then suddenly she said *goodbye* and got out and went into a nearby café, where someone was impatiently waiting for her.

A day later I phoned the woman who had been about to step on the rose of the soul who occupied my thoughts, no matter how I tried to avoid it — and I asked her to meet. Today the café terrace I was so fond of seemed unbearable. We left.

Imagine my utter surprise as I was crossing Jungmannovo Square when I saw about thirty steps away, her, whom I wasn't supposed to see until a week later. She was with her boyfriend. She suddenly noticed me. Her eyes! Her gestures! I said hello with a chuckle. Her face leapt toward me, she waved, ah, what confused gestures! Yet it's impolite to look back for too long.

When suddenly confronted with the reality of having to say goodbye, then all our old scabby anxieties open their hardened clam-like shells and, gripping the heart, this ingrate muscle, create havoc in us, as if we were saying goodbye forever.

I do not mean at all to imply that each great change that transports me anywhere beyond the world in which I live and submit to small benign changes is an agony for me, a painful death.

Now the time has come, in two or three days, for me to leave the sweet, lovely changes this book comprises, when my steps will take me somewhere different to be a Prague flâneur in exile, elsewhere, in a different city amid different walls.

Now the time has come, in two or three days, for me also — embarrassingly — to speak the word *farewell*. This quandary only intensifies my appalling insecurity, which always accompanies such a fateful *goodbye*, an insecurity I've carried inside my whole life.

No, I will not walk up Petřín Hill to take one last look from above of that "herd of bridges," the Vltava and both banks, the roofs of Old and New Town, the palaces of Malá Strana. I will not take the ferry at Troja to climb up the hillside to the house that was my prison for three years, to peer over it through the hawthorns at Prague right at the moment when all the women are making beds and the first pieces of kindling begin to flicker in their stoves. I will not walk higher from here to the town of the deranged to have its unexpected tower appear to me in the setting sun like a mirage over a February Sunday debacle. I will not take the road to Kobylisy just so I can greet from a distance with tumultuous and mellow heart a single small window still aglow — almost always a single one — behind which are several of my books and a woman who waits for me daily.

I will not stroll with her in the evening among the gardens of Troja, with the cherry trees in blossom, nor link arms with her to walk in a snowstorm on New Year's Eve, so dreary and marvelous, across a new bridge toward town just starting to incandesce, to a bar where a little piggy toddles. I will not go from there at evening to the abattoir to be astonished by the streetlights and the proximity of an alien city.

I will not walk to Stromovka Park, not in the morning to encounter two or three walkers nor in the afternoon to read Whitman's *Leaves of Grass*, nor on more distant afternoons to wander down the path from the office to opposite the rose bushes darkening with dusk and far from the blaring band to read *Manon Lescaut* or "Aladdin and His Magic Lamp."

I will not climb up the hill to make love to someone who has vanished from my sight forever, the sounds of a funeral march so close. I will not take a crowded tram from here with that same Lost Soul, full of blithe certainty that Jiří Wolker is waiting for me in a Smíchov tavern.

I will not go to the Kinský Garden in search of a kiss, nor to resist one, nor to greet the morning birds, nor to return from anywhere. I will not go into a Smíchov charcuterie with the voracious appetite of the eternal student, nor even into that cozy room where I crawled through the window to proclaim my love to a friend and listen to Mahler's *Songs on the Death of Children*, to this ground-floor room where Jiří Wolker and I improvised on piano with four hands — and where I was once visited by an angel.

I will not return at night to Na Celné Street to inform my Dadaist friends in the room below my tiny cell that Josef Kolínský has just been executed. Nor will I stand titillated outside the door of a woman sleeping with her nightshirt hiked up, nor will I wait there for the one with whom I wanted to die. I will not be at a hotel far from here awaiting my beloved misfortune so that I may go inside to drink cherry liqueur or sweet Graves wine, which even today I cannot taste without my heart being seized by angst.

I will not walk opposite other sites of sad delight to gaze with André Breton at a butterfly cocooned in a crystal globe. I will not be in a dive at Smíchov Station to hear the confessions of someone with nothing left to do but to die. I will no longer take the riverboat *Mayor Dietrich* to Zbraslav with tender heart, nor will I crane over the boat in which no one is waiting for me on a Sunday morning in spring.

I will not walk along Prague's bridges on the day of my parting with "Chimera," nor will I visit that obscure tiny wine bar so suffused with sorrow it brings tears to your eyes, and neither will I chase the phantoms of women on Rybná Street and go with them to the little rooms where they set aside their breasts.

I will not accompany André Breton and his wife to the Hotel Paris. I will not go with him and Paul Eluard into the wine bar on Old Town Square. I will not love the early spring twilight in the Klementinum courtyard. Escorting my beloved from my bed, I will not see Salvátorská Street to have the sight of the ice-cream shop give me the illusion of being in Italy.

I will not suffer the squalor and fading of love in a raftsmen's pub near Štefánik Bridge. I will not stand in delight before the Hotel Bavaria, where, as I dreamt it, Guillaume Apollinaire slept. I will not go with Jiří Wolker and

Konstantin Biebl to U Leflérů near Malostranské Square where the poet of "The Heresiarch" saw the Eternal Jew dance.

I will no longer greet Jiří Karásek ze Lvovic at the Malostranská Café nor at the Pigeons, and I will not impatiently count the hours there with the desire that the one I used to live for will walk through the door. I will not continue to the Napoleon, nor to Zbořenec, nor anywhere else to search in vain for my outlandish sensual dream.

I will not live in Karlín, in a cadaver room with my suitcase and read *Bubu of Montparnasse*, nor even below Vinohrady with the landlady who surprises me at the moment of ecstasy. Nor in Košíře in the room with an aquarium, on account of which I am awakened every day — and nude — by the whole family whose members were too numerous to count. Nor in the two houses on Moravská Street, in those two hapless homes. Nor in the Nusle Valley facing Botič Creek and eternal sadness. Nor on Sokolská Street, where my love teaches me how to reckon Tattva time. Nor in Troja or Střešovice across from the convent garden where nuns gather dry brushwood and dried laundry.

I either will or will not go to these and a thousand other places where my life, my fate, my love, my despair, my hope glitter with a joyous or sad light. Yet I will not go to say goodbye, because I fear goodbyes, they terrify me. I would never want to say goodbye at death's door.

I would rather dispel my anxiety instead and greet this or another morning star such as You, for whom I wait. And even if I do not live to see You, even if You do not come, even if your unsymbolic *farewell*, which we say out of habit, were a portend, I would still wish to greet You, to greet You for everything, everything for which I left home at odd hours so I could see a new, moving, visible correspondence of unexpected images, unexpected associations. Everything for which I have abandoned my thinking and habits to learn minor variations, those small marvelous variations in which poetry resides.

For all my loves and for Prague, through which I walked with their lanterns, their wandering eyes, their fire or boredom, their shoes.

And if our meeting chance had bestowed on me was for no other reason than to revive in me a modicum of delight or nostalgia, then let it be You for whom I have lived so many minutes, so many hours, more fevered than I lived without You, for whom my steps became more errant, my words more fervent, my waiting more intense than without You.

But if You should come, then let it be neither to stay nor to say goodbye. For — and this I know, I feel — for — this I wish — that when the final word brings this book to a close you'll see me exit its end somewhere above or below to the streets where chance will once again unite us, once again separate us — and where, without anyone hearing me utter a word, I am and will remain for all time a Prague flâneur.

Where has the time gone from the moment I finished writing the previous lines as dusk fell on the afternoon of July 7, 1937, to the moment when an October evening in a café with bare windows, having enticed me to transpose the area of Prague between the Parliament and Štefánik Bridge to Leningrad and the Winter Palace, pressed the quill into my hand? Where has the time gone!

Its plume is blown between the pines of several summer solitudes where the hair of the woman who indulged my presence transforms into the gold of an Indian summer. The cities that have witnessed the unintended pauses afflicting this book, the cities with arcades and hotels facing churches, saw this pair of exiles gaze evening after evening above the roofs of perpetual change, above the vistas of streets, to which we do not return, at always the same conjunction of Venus and Mars.

How could I have added, either there or elsewhere, or in one of the world's most foreign cities, whose postal building commanded all my attention as painters worked on it for nearly three whole months, a single line to a book whose contours long ago seemed to be formed of my past and dreams, whose seeds have long since been swallowed by the wind?

I have never thought it necessary to enter my book through the gates of the present moment, as is the case with these pages, on whose long abandoned blank surface a sidereal tear from my female companion, like a supreme talisman, has just dropped. That I did not hesitate to say goodbye was all for nothing — fortunately! And my steps are no longer mine. Invisible chance will no longer be my guide, either kind or unkind, albeit always the marvelous consoler of the solitary.

And what would be the point of this whole goggle-eyed pursuit of its fantastic revelations (a white bird flutters over the Vltava long before we register that spring has arrived) if the discoveries we have made our own are to be consecrated to the ebb like a wave, if chance, at the moment it is the scorching blast of a brilliant rocket tracing our signature, were not miraculously fixed in what we have learned, happily and fatally learned and greeted as necessity.

And so from the moment when my steps are no longer mine, when the footprints of tomorrow and the future are determined and guided by my love for a being who fills me with hope that it will not dissolve into mirage, from the moment when my steps have echoed the footsteps of Diana, what I have called the poetry of minor variations is revealed to me in the entrancing light of an aimless walk, which is life itself.

If it is solitude you seek, then upon entering cafés such as the Old Demínka or the Paris Café you'll be taken aback in the same way as by the liveliest Prague streets dimly lit as prescribed by air defense drills. The entire tableau shifts several years into the past.

In certain express ironing shops, where I was obliged to spend fifteen minutes in a cubicle, I would normally witness, in a rather animated state, my transference to a past that owed its existence to the outmoded sketches of dandies who, along with the carriages they leaned against, belonged to a bygone age still remembered by an armoire or two.

It was just such a transference of Prague to fifteen years earlier that was evoked by those cafés in my mind's eye. Everything was as it had been then, the oppressive atmosphere, several students studying for their graduation exams, pensioners, elderly women sipping coffee, and something ineffably Prague-like, bursting with prewar bohemianism, several devotees of which I got to know in the years immediately following the overthrow of the government, when I would visit the Tůmovka and the Unionka, and when Prague still had a plethora of cafés similar to the Paris Café and the Old Demínka.

In such cafés you would be sure to see V.H. Bruner in the company of literati who had a special and intimately waggish relationship with the hoary headwaiters who, adhering to august tradition, regaled them with a steady stream of jokes along with their newspapers and black coffee.

Besides, all of Bruner's celebrated caricatures of amorous scenes in notebooks passing from hand to hand among the customers whom the headwaiter deemed worthy of his trust will soon be entirely forgotten. Whenever I read Jaroslav Hašek's stories, I am returned in spirit to these cafés whose last Mohicans, a little despondent by the passing of those who constituted their fame, still retain that familiar, slightly fusty ambience of anarchist humor despite the winged years flapping away, and if Jindřich Hořejší no less has moved on from them, it just reflects the fact that the link to their era of glory has been ruptured, the times have changed, and these forgotten cafés have become the stuff of legend today, resurrected only in poetry.

And yet, the Tůmovka was exactly one of those watering holes of the marvelous in which aging prewar bohemians and the young avant-garde generation formed a chain that, contrary to appearances, was never entirely broken, never entirely ruptured.

Whenever I chance to set foot in the Old Deminka, the

Paris Café, and the Tůmovka, the illusion is revived in me that time has stood still, that I have not aged, that Jiří Wolker is still alive, that the city is not falling under the sway of that generic international style adopted by all the new cafés, that there is peace, that to speak of war is nonsense, crazy talk, that only now has life begun in Prague.

It was on another day, when I was invited to attend a meeting at Café Slovanka, that I was allowed to spontaneously forget the passing of time and to witness the preparations for seminars and degree exams that occupied the students sitting there.

Here, right here, just as in the several cafés I have already mentioned, is where Prague lives, untouched by the transformations to her appearance and mores that have been taking place over the past years before my very eyes, unrecognizably similar to the one that saw me wandering around the scattered university lecture halls — and the one I heard about from friends, who two decades before me undertook the same errant path of hunger.

One December day in 1920 I dined as the guest of Jiří Mahen in a charcuterie on Spálená Street, and as his animated presence and words related his memories, I was transported once and for all to this charcuterie circa 1905, and since that day I sometimes like to stop in here, like entering certain prewar books. And, so moved, I always see Prague extending her hand sheathed in a glove from 1905, always let myself be moved by the allure of things lost, just as in Café Slovanka by the strange, ageless, drab, touching silhouettes of those bowed over lectures, in most cases delivered today by graybeards who see present life only through the lens of what was and whose poetic sensibilities are rather close to this café of silhouettes.

While accompanying me there, Jan Mukařovský told me he remembered this café from his student years, and I regretted he couldn't go in right then to confirm for me that my appreciation of such oases where Prague has resisted her total transformation is not purely subjective, as it might seem, that these oases do indeed exist, and that the nostalgia I feel whenever that clammy, moldy, and yet so genial, so genuine freshness wafts over me is part of the invisible rosary of links that form a tradition.

Like those decolorized gravies whose ashen odor would obscure the sky over me in the courtyard of the former university canteen on Spálená Street, this café of silhouettes reminded me that what is called the happy life of a student is still even today battered by the rainstorms of indigence, by the depressively splenetic fear of tomorrow, by the dust of studies so bitter, so saturated with the chilly hoarfrost of cramped student chambers.

And the awareness that in a land where the proletariat is victorious the student is no longer an evil who has to be subsidized, whose uselessness requires swift dispensation, but instead is a member of the self-assured army of workers, brought a sigh and stirred my desire to make a promise from the future that the "bewitching" atmosphere I found in the Slovanka be destined for extinction and shift from the realm of life and reality solely into the realm of poetry.

And you, my sweet guide, whom I saw as I entered the café

of silhouettes with head bent over a book, you, girl from a different time, one so close to my present passions, you, for whom so much archaic charm is no longer comprehensible, though still captivating to me, you could not suspect that this special type of sorrow constituting a student's existence, this onerous sorrow you would like to escape (O how I understand you!) marked my youth with the very same song of the barrel organ that has assumed the right to so insistently sadden your days.

How I would've liked to take your hand and lead you away from this murky nest of spidery patience to a balcony with a horizon bright and pure that would empower your miraculous abilities so they would not need to withdraw before the imperious finger of study pressing at your temple.

How dreary those long years tied to tutorials and bereft of hope, how long they were! How I wished for you, for all those young shadows, bent over the obligation to renunciation and self-sacrifice, that those years might be shortened by a miraculous wager on a single card, that those years, rolled up in a diploma, could be filed in the very bottom of your trunk.

Sadly though, this era, in the grips of a crisis far worse than the years I was transported to by Café Slovanka, is shuttering that bright horizon before you — what misery! And though the road you are condemned to travel leads to the desolate dance halls of social destitution, it is still possible to move off it, away from its ink-stained milestones, by a liberating gesture, a gesture arising from my chest when crossing over the threshold of this café out to the street where, alas!, the hazy day of social turmoil quivered.

And similar to how the streets of Vinohrady at the moment I was walking them, dejected by a sleepless night, vividly brought to my mind the wretched little rooms in which I so desperately felt the bondage, socially and humanly, of my fettered youth, this café touched me and made me wistful, filling me with tenderness and melancholy.

How grateful I am to you that I did go in! That my love, so sovereignly conjuring up rapture, was allowed this walk on which I encounter, on which I encountered, many young, many no longer young, many now aged and sensitive beings who either side with me, or who, unless they have somehow managed to shed their confining, spurious Inverness, condemn me, impugn me, repudiate me.

I have nearly wholly abnegated any desire to decide where the wind shall direct my steps. My reward is to witness unexpected entries into places that with the passing of so much time have become very distant from the terrain on which my conscious possibilities move, granting me a dream, a peek at a film not pre-staged on any page I take in hand.

It was neither my choice nor need, paid for by self-denial, that opened the gates of the old St. Thomas Brewery, and on a Saturday no less, when its cellar tavern is at its liveliest. Someone walking through the quiet evening streets around Malostranské Square would hardly realize that close by is a place where, huddled cheek by jowl, young and old, men and women form a mob, which if pressed together like this on one of the neighboring squares would be the picture of a demonstration, and one hardly arousing any concern at that since why this faceless throng had gathered to demonstrate would not be difficult to fathom though unclear under what banner.

When I saw the eruptions of glee or rancor from this boisterous mass, united at first sight by nothing more than pints of the dark beer that is a staple of this tavern, I couldn't help but recall a particular description of Adolf Hitler's first forays into political agitation, how he started in the cellar of a Munich beerhall similar to the cellar of the St. Thomas Brewery. Yes, it might have been among an amorphous crowd such as this that Hitler bagged his first modest game, the consequences of which have turned out to be so catastrophic.

There is nothing so dangerous as the faceless masses doomed to a steady erosion of their beery merriment without having been led to a true consciousness of the causes for their social situation. Such a mass, left too long to the mercies of uncontrollable influences and to its own helpless desire to claim a slice of an erstwhile prosperity that has considerably dwindled during the years of economic crisis, such a mass, already aggrieved to the point of discontent and not yet driven into fold of the social framework where the proletariat is resident and conscious, constituted the first cadre for Hitler's demagoguery and today constitutes the most suitable material in the hands of contortionists with a socioeconomic system on the verge of collapse.

Thinking up a few slogans and trying to guess which would be the quickest to take root in this beer-soaked company all but confirmed my belief that those of fascism would be the ones greeted with the greatest enthusiasm.

For the discontent and the resentment of those who are

losing benefits — albeit meager but real all the same — create fertile ground for each and every more absurd, chauvinistic, debasing racial ideology over sober reflection that would acknowledge stark reality and not indulge antiquated perversions of it — thereby recognizing the existence of the class struggle.

Who knows where the wire conveying the scourge of fascist thought from one beerhall to the next leads, a scourge that to everyone's shock during the elections a few years back confronted us with the astounding fact that a party suffused with fascist ideology gained in Prague of all places an astonishing number of votes.

When I observed that faceless, jabbering mass drinking dark St. Thomas beer, I couldn't help but see them as the source even today of that outdated mentality found in Ignát Herrmann's quaint little figures, who on such a menacing scale still populate Czech films, as both the inspiration for and the consumer of these films, and how this particular mentality reinforces the burgeoning fascism. The excessive abstraction of thought in today's political journalism and the excess of abstraction in the schematic realism that has crept into contemporary social novels have veiled the true and active strata of the reactionary processes engendering fascism, the reactionary processes that have so palpably found fertile ground in a place such as the St. Thomas brewpub.

It's unfortunate that in the hours when Malá Strana is still asleep a midnight miasma proliferating in these cellars drifts to all corners of the town, under roofs where it will become invisible. To someone who encounters such a mob it might seem as if nothing's afoot. And if of a sentimental bent, then

PHOTO : V. NEZVAL

I have nearly wholly abnegated any desire to decide where the wind shall direct my steps. p. 48

this or that old Prague song might spring to mind. Nothing more.

And meanwhile certain reactionary evening newspapers are living off this beer-fueled mentality with increasing circulation, living off it and leering in delight at these hidden, very well hidden, reserves of theirs, at first glance seeming so true to Prague and her former mores.

As I was leaving the St. Thomas Brewery, which is such a poetic sight, so much from another era, so satisfying to its customers, I had the impression that beyond the goodwill I wish for the people of Prague I had just uncovered a storehouse with crates of weapons and explosives labeled, *Made in Germany, Made in Italia, Made in Japan*.

Where has this book of mine been hiding since I lost track of it in one of the small squares of Malá Strana preparing for winter hibernation? May the order governing the setting sun and subterranean rivers not allow this book to again forsake the ground beneath my feet! Spring, chasing with braided whip my desire, which has a date with me on every street, this spring is here, this spring has set out its two tables on the sidewalk of Újezd Street with the promise that any ramble fate has in store for me will no longer chain me to the white pillar of rueful gazing into the distance.

The urgent letter that arrived on December 4, 1937, and called me to my mother's bedside brought a sudden end to my excursions along Prague's stairs. With what awe I awaited spring, having seen it enter the city's medieval streets — which I have haunted for many years like a blind sibyl from the age of marionettes — in my most avid dreams, in which all my hopes and all my faith in the marvelous have been placed. With what awe I awaited it and how fervently I pressed my lips to its hand clad in a lace glove now covered by a single bracelet : the malachite dome of the Church of St. Nicholas off which the sun has just moved.

Everything that has happened had to happen for me to be placed before my book nearly at the midpoint of the same walk I began a year ago and whose final steps I have yet to see, whose trailing echo I have yet to hear.

At the moment I wished to make *A Prague Flâneur* the companion and conclusion to *Invisible Moscow* and *Rue Gît-le-Coeur* I certainly had no inkling that every single theme in either of these two books would no longer be germane, and that I would have no reason to circle back to them now, as I was intending, that not even one of the themes of those two books would be carried to conclusion.

After midnight, on March 7, 1938, I visited one of those nightspots on National Avenue, which, as I learned when I first came to Prague, was frequented by those whom I once considered friends, for whom, their table society scattered for years, I set in motion the wheel of the Surrealist mill four years ago, and from whom I have now been estranged for several months.

This meeting, at which I had promised to clarify my position on some contentious issues (primarily of a political nature arising from the current international situation and concerns over the trials of the Trotskyist-Bukharinite opposition in the Soviet Union), a position at odds with that of the other members of the Surrealist Group, turned into a rather heated altercation between myself and those whom for years I had never stopped placing in the light of my dream, whom for years I had engaged as participants in the theatrical performance staged by my desire.

I prefer not to chronicle this scene in which I was cast in the role of opposition against all my erstwhile friends, the day ending with our split.

Considering that on the final pages of *Rue Gît-le-Coeur* I lament that after a chance encounter with André Breton on Pont du Carrousel, which for both of us seemed a manifestation of the marvelous, I did not accompany him to the left bank of the Seine — and if in my devoted affection for him I regretted that at the time when the Surrealist Group in Czechoslovakia was to sign onto his manifesto "On the Time When the Surrealists Were Right" I could not add my signature for imperatively objective reasons — I observed with deep sorrow that after the Moscow trials, to which Breton's *opposition* was absolutely categorical, a chasm had opened between his position on the matter and the position that I inevitably came to after a thorough study of the Radek Trial, and in light of my emotional attachment to him, I was distressed at the thought that it was highly unlikely this chasm could ever be filled in, or skirted, or bridged.

While on a rainy day in the first pages of this book I was searching in the speech Bukharin delivered at the All-Union Congress of Soviet Writers for clues to what might have landed him in a Soviet prison, and while on March 7, 1938, the day of the split between me and my former friends, a day when it was abundantly clear that Bukharin's life was over, I couldn't help but see with regret (this was a man who had commanded my absolute trust at the All-Union Congress) and anger (was the treason committed by Bukharin and his accomplices not the most devastating betrayal ever in history?) that all those words he spoke at the Congress, which primarily impressed the delegates from the West, were nothing more than a lure to catch that oddly sensitive and oddly callous fish known as the intellectual!

Given the pain and anger I felt the moment I understood the incontrovertible authenticity of the Moscow trials and realized how the Trotskyist and Bukharinite conspirators had intended to endanger socialism, and (if I were to consider the pressing conditions of our lives and the city whose arcana have guided me for several years) how the conspirators were gambling with all our fates, it was natural that I would look to those closest to me to empathize with my pain and anger.

While I rationalized to myself Breton's uncompromising opposition to the Moscow trials and the politics of the Soviet Union as being on the one hand consistent with the age-old tradition prevalent in the artistic milieu of Montmartre to revolt against *any kind* of conformism while being on the other hand an emotional response provoked by the unfair treatment he received from the majority of French intellectual workers in the communist camp who had prevented him from delivering his planned speech at the Congress of Writers in Paris after his run-in with Ehrenburg — and while I am indeed aware that Paris is further west than Prague and feels less acutely the existential danger of an imminent attack by Nazi Germany — I have tried to understand his misguided position, admittedly highly subjective, on the Soviet Union's present policies and the ongoing trials there. Yet I did not expect those who live in the same conditions as I, those whose circumstances predispose them to experience contemporary history in the same way as I, would be so utterly deaf to objective arguments and let their incomprehension of the present historical moment turn each exchange between us on current events into a dispute that revealed after a few sentences that we are no longer, nor could ever be, friends.

Considering the response to the countless examples I provided to underscore that *my* friendship was shown through my actions brutally laid bare the essence of those who for so long had earned my trust, insofar as they deemed it an opportune moment to so acrimoniously express their animus to me, then this has doubtlessly been a long-standing sentiment just skillfully concealed and masked.

While to this day they have made no attempt to clarify for me what aspects of my activity they found objectionable, and given they had asked me to introduce the Toyen and Štyrský exhibition at Salon Topič in January 1938 and were likely aware of my sweeping lecture on Surrealism on February 11 at the Masaryk Public Education Institute, their sudden hostility that broke out in the open on March 7 was in sharp contrast with the friendship I had extended to them and with their attitude toward me prior to this day.

While I, too, am prone to emotional overreaction, I have no reason to make too much of spats among friends resulting from such outbursts — and I'm not in the habit of holding a grudge for long against those I love for any offense that is a common byproduct of such friendly squabbles.

This time, the objective reasons underlying this conflict, and the rancor and extreme animosity directed at me, were proof enough that I needed to wake up from my dream of friendship, which I had so ardently nourished, that the fable of friendship I had conceived with the whole of my desire was over, that I needed to admit to myself what I had long resisted, and I would have to reevaluate the true nature and actual character of those I had associated with my dream.

I experienced another awkward situation on March 9 when I was awakened by the postman with a letter for me, written in the wooden style of an urgent business matter, which inquired if I still considered myself a member of the Surrealist Group.

I didn't take umbrage at having this question put to me — if I still considered myself a member of the group I myself had founded — by those I had made great effort to bring together and to lead, despite the seeming impossibility of it. Aware that it was incumbent on me to express with all sovereignty my sense of responsibility for my own creation, that very afternoon I picked up the phone and called the editors of *Haló News* to deliver a short, succinct statement to run in the newspaper's early edition the same day that I had dissolved the hitherto Surrealist Group in Czechoslovakia.

Anyone who has read *Invisible Moscow* and *Rue Gît-le-Coeur* knows of my ardent feelings for André Breton and can well imagine the pain I experienced upon realizing I would need to inform my friend of the schism, that I needed to, even if only cursorily without delving into all the excruciating details, apprise him of the situation and the circumstances behind it.

I sent the letter on March 9, and writing it was the most distressing aspect of the whole affair, but at the same time I knew that my determination to block all possible avenues for my own emotions to interfere in the matter, a determination to take a strictly objective position, precluded both any backsliding in my feelings for my erstwhile friends as well as exacting any sort of revenge on them.

Our dispute was fundamental, and I wasn't about to let it somehow become the plaything of subjective forces. It was a dispute that required from me strict objectivity with all its consequences and without any deviation even if, as could be expected, my former friends would not shrink from attacking this objectivity. It should have been resolved in public, and the most crucial questions discussed as openly as possible, even at the risk of subjecting myself to attacks from those who have no comprehension of revolutionary truth.

In any case, their attack was not long in coming — that it was launched by those who view hostility toward the Soviet Union as their life's mission brought me some satisfaction — and appeared in the *Evening News*, *Express*, and the *Sunday Gazette* exactly at the same time when Hitler was entering Vienna.

After these attacks from avowed adherents of fascist tactics, a notice appeared in the dailies stating that my expulsion from the Surrealist Group was unanimous. I furnished *Haló News* with a short text that detailed the objective reasons for the schism.

A sense of propriety keeps me from mentioning any of the efforts made by the members of the Surrealist Group to discredit me, behind my back, which I always learned of in short order. For that matter, I was prepared for their whisper campaign, since their diatribes against me lacked any sort of objectivity. By virtue of a vacuous little article that ran in the *Morning News*, and, as I came to learn, the calumnies spread about me by my onetime friends, I announced that in the future I would not be responding to any of their public or surreptitious innuendoes.

On March 20, I received a long and rather amicable letter from André Breton. The letter's postscript implied that my former friends had given the primary reason for the schism as their disapproval of three of my poems whose subject was T.G. Masaryk on the one hand and Stalin on the other. Why, then, did they not chastise me for these poems in their article attacking me in the *Morning News*, and why in their pamphlet from the end of May is their criticism focused mainly on the formal aspects of my Masaryk poems, which by way of Breton they indirectly requested I disavow? Did they not realize as they were denouncing me to Breton for my Masaryk poems, which were a reaction to a singular historical moment affecting us all, that he, not being conversant with the history and politics of Czechoslovakia and lacking understanding of the situation in which we were living, would view these poems as nothing more than incidental verse about a king? Was it courage that prevented the members of my former group from giving the Czechoslovak public the same rationale they gave to Breton for objecting to my Masaryk poems?

I waited a long time before replying to Breton, and not because I couldn't find the words, but because I was putting off the moment when in spite of myself I would have to sadden him. Relying on his singular sensibility, relying on his full understanding of my distaste for relaying all the embarrassing details of the whole contentious affair, I wrote him a very friendly letter in broad brushstrokes, with a minimum of pathos, in which I clarified that what he had termed my resignation in his letter and what I had taken exception to was now water under the bridge as far as I was concerned.

In a second letter to Breton I wrote that I considered my position on the schism as definitive. In no way did I make any attempt to relitigate the dispute nor did I care to address any lingering issues.

Whereas Benjamin Péret informed me that it was conveyed to him by the members of the Surrealist Group that I had regressed to writing proletarian poetry, and whereas he stated that I had offered no counterarguments against them in my letter and requested that I make a "gesture" that would allow a relationship to be reestablished between me and them, who, as I should be aware, have no qualms at all about producing accusations against me, and whereas I ultimately learned secondhand from Paris that the members of the Prague Surrealist Group had been sending to Paris ample "material" against me, I made it clear to Péret that I had no intention to respond to arguments whose validity I could not judge until I was given a chance to review all of the damning "material" being circulated.

• • •

Some might think the way I approached this rift, at least with regard to the French Surrealists, involved somewhat extraneous considerations on my part.

Given that the interpretation of reality in a way that

singularly embodies revelation through imagination is part of my own distinctive method, which I have utilized in my poetry from my very first collection, I saw no need, as some have challenged me to do, to haggle with anyone over this method, even if it were someone who has done more than anyone else to develop the idea of Surrealism, even if it were André Breton himself. Given that in *Communicating Vessels* he felt no compunction about judging, and sometimes rather harshly, Freud, his mentor to whom the greater part of his insights were indebted, then why should someone act any differently in a similar situation?

And while I did ask Breton for his blessing to my continuing to lead Surrealist activities in Czechoslovakia in his name with people for whom such activity, in my judgment, would mean more than it did for the so-called "majority of the Czech Surrealist Group," this request was not made in the belief that further evolution of the idea required authorization from the person who had launched it into orbit, nor was it made to seek any extrinsic benefit from such authorization. It was, instead, an expression of my commitment to the main tenets of this idea and to those who had so fervently devoted themselves to it, and not for any organizational reasons, which, after all, have their own unique conditions in each part of the world, the same febrile exhilaration of the marvelous that guided my steps in 1933 to the café at Place Blanche.

This might be an opportune moment for me to revise the conception of friendship I had elaborated in *Invisible Moscow* and *Rue Gît-le-Coeur*, as a corrective to my innate desire to view friendship in the light of legend, given that the majority of those who were the recipients of my devotion in those two books are no longer my friends.

I will not do it. I cannot do it. For as I write this, new bells have begun to ring in the mountains. These bells, these bells of a desire that wants to outlast the ultimate disappointment, whose essence is that it outlasts the ultimate disappointment, ring from town to town and call one another to form a great vertiginous chorus. Of those who shake hands at my door, some return with eyes beguiled by dream.

Ah, if this retinue, great or small, of the like-minded who might bring reinforcement does not impede understanding between individuals and the collective, then why would not, why should not, one after another ascend the stairs entranced into that epically dazzling magnesium light that epitomizes the endless desire to live time more passionately, life more passionately, as two, as five, as twenty, in the constant yearning for harmony with millions.

And even if the table of winter should topple over a hundred times on our desire, it would not be hindered from omnipotently seeking its gratification, no matter how futile, no matter how impossible, nor would it hinder the poet who wishes, dares, feels compelled to sustain the breathtaking vigor of this desire, its awesome, tantalizing, magical power!

And you, city, so long veiled in mist and sleet before my eyes, you, city, whom I emotionally remember in a moment of anguish over her, forever irreplaceable, whom no other human being could ever equal in the eyes of my desire, in anguish over her life, her love, and her still unruffled brow, you, city, whose exile and son I am, today you would have me forget that time passes, that a year has passed, that this spring, this summer, are not the same ones on whose doorsteps I penned the first lines of this book.

It is evening and I'm sitting alone in the places where my last year's desire listened in the depths of night for the clatter of heels, lifted by the little wings of Mercury. Your steps draw near. I hear them and a voice that used to be theirs, and is theirs again. Let it come from the cold, let it come from privation, fatigue, the noisy streets, the dust that is no longer my dust. It comes to carry me off (oh, where to, where to!), to circuitously lead me around myself, around my solitary self, to guide me to all those places where I am a Prague flâneur. I hear it — and my gratitude, my eyes turning to the river into which the city pours an endless stream of tears from its dark womb, hears above and below the fading tones of a dulcimer (or has it only now begun to ring).

How could I not reserve a place in these pages for the images of Prague I carry around in my mind, only I alone (just as we alone carry in our thoughts the resplendence of night, fully belying the night, when we sleep, and as a raven carries its experience from the land where we heard it croak and appear nevermore), for those images that were a gift to me beyond talent, when I least expected it, images in which I felt myself to be an accidental witness to situations profoundly subjected to what Freud termed dreamwork.

This recasting could only happen after it took me a few years, and under the exhausting circumstances duty had set before me, to become acquainted with the Prague streets and neighborhoods, after suffering dreary bouts of depression from places that meant nothing, could mean nothing, to me.

While in April 1920 I found myself adrift in the deluge of apartment houses so ill-suited to the fascinating name of Prague, lost in this deluge through my nostalgia for the towns where I had left behind my short and stormy history, nothing my gaze encountered was so alluring to suggest that Prague was beautiful, that she enchanted me, that I loved her.

While Czech poetry, the paltry pages that inspired me, furnished scant few inviting localities in Prague where I could wander with the excitement of a young musician on his way to attend his first opera he has only read and dreamed about, while this poetry, via Machar and Sova, put in a seductive light only Stromovka Park, Žofín, and that Magdalene from the cabaret to which I would migrate from the moment the red eyes of the Black Cat lit up the corner of Rybná Street, what attracted me more in this poetry were the city's creatures than Prague herself.

Prague trams conveyed me from the realms of apathy to the realms of the marvelous on the day a tall brown-haired man in a black wide-brimmed hat got on at the Myslíkova stop who might have been the anarchist writer Fráňa Šrámek, whose poetry collection *The Weir* and novel *Body* had such an emotional impact on me then — and a short time later when I encountered in a tram car a woman with whom I'd once been madly in love.

This rather disagreeable means of transportation became somewhat emotionally vindicated in my eyes on the day I saw in Malá Strana not far from the Štefánik Barracks a bakery

PHOTO : V. NEZVAL

While it didn't take long for me to be roused by the louche alleyways of Old Town . . . p. 66

from an angle that transported me to one Sunday afternoon in a small town near a house with a panorama.

While it didn't take long for me to be roused by the louche alleyways of Old Town where I pursued my idealized Magdalene, I only became reconciled to my squalid little room in Karlín on the evening I returned home directly from a Lantern Festival over the Vltava — and once there, presumably under the sway of the Lantern Festival which had so fired my imagination, I became aware that in the next room a married couple, staying the night as guests of my landlord, were making love, arousing me as I let the first pages of *Bubu of Montparnasse* transport me to Rue de Grenelle the day after the 14th of July holiday.

From that day on, the dirty little room occupied by Bubu and Berthe turned my wretched hovel into something voluptuous, since its very wretchedness was what opened a space inside me where some of Berthe's girlfriends could enter, if not Berthe herself, just returning from her father's funeral clad in mourning dress.

So my *Bubu of Montparnasse* enacted in the gray desolate lanes of Prague made Karlín bearable, whose poetic essence, once engendered in me by Gustav Pfleger Moravský's social novel and now in the thrall of Charles-Louis Philippe, received a new, ultra-vibrant source of inspiration. Ultimately another source of light illuminated the dismal, sunless melancholy of my bleak abode — letters from my friend Jiří Mahen, which allowed me to nourish the illusion that I am a poet.

Because the poet Karel Hlaváček had walked its streets, I was in love with the Libeň district even before the moment, on my way to visit his grave, I discovered in the window of a small bookshop a long out-of-print edition of one of his collections. I came to idolize Libeň and was overcome with excitement when a few years later I learned that the woman of my dreams came from this very same suburb.

It's a shame that in not one of the three places I lived in Vinohrady, nor in Košíře, nor Smíchov, nor in the Nusle Valley, did an intermediary appear either in my imagination or in a literary work whose salutary magic would enable me to bear with at least a modicum of poetic ecstasy the penurious living conditions that shackled me in those places. Not until the dream from the first canto of my poem *Edison* did I feel the need, and long after I had moved away from those locales, to illuminate Košíře myself through the unreal guide my imagination had encountered on Legion Bridge.

And while I eventually came to acknowledge the poetic charm of Smíchov, I would first have to travel to Paris to remember this Prague district so long silent to me in Montparnasse. And if on the day we met I accompanied to Vinohrady the woman who's already traversed this book so that on the way back, now alone with a desire for love, I could see Mírové Square bathed in dazzling light, which to my eyes lent the city a romantic strangeness, I would have to take a hundred random detours before I was able to hear, and without these inspirational aids, Prague start to play her elaborate organ.

So during a foggy, muddy Sunday in February 1927 when my girlfriend and I went out for a walk, leaving the cottage in the Troja neighborhood where I spent my days, to climb up to the fields swept with bleak hoarfrost, I suddenly saw in the red glow of the setting sun, as if by a miracle, the tower of the

Bohnice psychiatric hospital, its unexpected appearance so galvanizing that after returning to my garret in Troja I wrote the third canto to *Acrobat* that very same evening, and often climbing from then on to the top of the hill above the cottage to hypnotically gaze at the distant lights of Prague. The moment I saw Prague from this vantage on one of my morning strolls through the freshly blooming pink hawthorn it occurred to me that behind each one of the thousands of morning Prague windows were a thousand girls draped in hawthorn aprons, young housewives making the bed. I was delighted by the thought of stepping through all those windows and surprising all those lovely young ladies with a sprig of hawthorn.

A similar feeling possessed me, although one situated in the depths of night, when I once unexpectedly came into nighttime Prague by car from a city where I had seen a very moving stage performance. Because so unanticipated, these two tremendous embraces by Prague commanded my fascination all the more than do the vistas from atop Petřín Hill, which are in someways predestined just by the act of walking up it.

I shall not speak of gardens and palaces, places where the rising and setting sun forever and always meanders to intersect our lives where its most sensitive, to miraculously rearrange the contents of the drawers in that mysterious armoire from the highest to the lowest.

This might be why I was so happy to visit the Kinský Garden and connect the most forlorn tip of Malá Strana with a small-town park where students were preparing for graduation exams a week before the end of the school year. Or maybe a little Košíře park brought me so much joy that after leaving at the end of the day a procession of tin advertisements for chicory in out-of-the-way shops would still appear to me a long time after.

If a gully swollen with the first spring runoff such as I saw in the most godforsaken places in Střešovice could illuminate for me with its genuineness those doleful and abstract spaces of new whitewashed buildings and excavated ground, how could I not notice the faded charm of some insignificant streets at the moment I saw a funeral procession wending its way through them.

If seeing a street such as Ruská Avenue with its garden villas (maybe for the first time in my life) on one of my aimless Sunday strolls produced in me the kind of derangement for which I have a boundless love, a derangement coinciding with dreamlike dislocations and countless others as well, which cannot be induced artificially, for which you have to wait, either a long or a short time, if it seemed to me when looking at the gardens on Ruská Avenue (it was springtime) that all the windows of these huge garden villas set back from the street were alight with glittering Christmas trees — and if I mention this particular sensation over others — then it should come as no surprise that I learned to love Prague at the moment she caught me unawares on the stage of disorientation, when she began to appear to me made over in surprising ways, when I became a Prague flâneur.

I was so inflamed with the impression that Ruská Avenue was part of a city I didn't know, in which I was a stranger, that I began to tremble in ecstasy even in the locality of the Vinohrady water tower, a place I know well, and I deliberately shut my eyes so that when I entered the studio of my friend, the painter Bedřich Vaníček, it would be in that city so unbelievably alien and in a time far removed from that Sunday, having just made my way to Král Jiří Square.

And if I'm allowed a hackneyed image, which contrary to expectations best captures my present mood, it seemed to me as if I were stepping into the studio from other lives somehow, or maybe as if in a play, a wonderstruck actor and spectator both.

I had a similar sensation another time when I came rather late to the Malvazinky Cemetery on the eve of All Souls' Day — and when I saw those thousands of little flames lighting up the dark and creating over Prague, into which I headed as if into the unknown, a city above the city. Or when at dusk at the end of a feast day I saw on the edge of Břevnov that a few of those lovely little shops were open, covering my eyes with their hands like a close friend whom I couldn't really identify when suddenly surprised like that.

For so long I was forced to live outside the center of Prague on its most incredible periphery, in those sparse neighborhoods where on returning home late at night I would meet with only a single lit window, behind which I would lie down in bed! For so long I was forced to look at this city as a distant All Souls' Day cemetery and guess by the map of lights where this or that beloved was sleeping, was just getting into bed, before I could feel that its streets were winged, that they uniquely corresponded to my dreams and possessed everything that might activate my dreaming.

To conclude, an aimless walk such as the one early on Christmas Eve that led me from Troja all the way to Karlín by a circuitous path through half of Prague to the novelty shops and the pastry shops with the pink and greenish charm of a rural konditorei, a walk that resulted in the purchase of an alarm clock, is one of those helpers who decided to rivet her gypsy eyes on me for so long that one day I discovered I was bewitched by Prague.

Before this book imbibes a few more drops of the sleeping potion made from cinnamon red surprises (although I'm especially fond of the indescribable brown of old window frames in the little houses under Charles Bridge near Dražický Square, where I was particularly taken with a small balcony for three suspended from a wine restaurant), and before I make another attempt to uncoil the snake of medieval turrets from around me, I would like to revise a number of principles I adopted as my own on the first pages of *Invisible Moscow* (as if my steps were not nearly always driven by inner impulses that in one way or another convincingly defined said principles), and, with eyes fixed on my present paths, confirm or refute a few fundamental ideas for which Surrealism has had a thing or two to say.

But first allow me to reference something Marx asserted, namely, his perfectly justifiable bias against "practical necessity," which he rightly saw as synonymous with avarice, to underscore that as a direct consequence of the universal blindness engendered by capitalism, having fetishized "practical necessity," human life and the productivity of the human spirit are valuated, even by those souls who have their sights on a more just future, far too exclusively by the degree to which they serve such "practical necessity."

Here (as it is useless to debate with the champions of capitalism) I'm referring to evaluating the activity of the human spirit in light of the practical necessity for revolution, which has already jolted the world because its aim is the very demise of capitalism, each in the dialectical grinder through which all things must pass, all phenomena related in some way to practical necessity qua avarice.

If intoxication is inarguably an emotional aspect of reality, which could be subsumed under the concept of dreaming, a most sublime beauty, one of the highest values of life, now understood outside the realm of practical necessity, that thousandfold avarice coloring the bourgeois pursuit of joy in life, if beauty derived from dreaming is a return to the most intrinsic domain of life, as it wishes to elevate itself to unprecedented heights via socialism, then we cannot avoid the question if dream is, or could be, as André Breton would have it, the father of action, or if there exists a terrain between dream and action whose excavation could be linked to the violent intervention of our will.

When discussing the word "action" let's not get sidetracked by classless society, the anticipation of which only triggers our impatience, but look instead for the content of "action" in everything, the heroic and unheroic, that falls within the purview of external exigency, whereupon for dream and dreaming we reserve a domain of the highest inner "freedom," a "freedom" that manifests only in this domain, which will presumably remain reserved even in a world where the sphere of external exigency is dialectically transformed into the sphere of external freedom.

To keep from dwelling too long in abstraction, allow me to quote Plato as paraphrased by Freud that, "The virtuous man contents himself with dreaming that which the wicked man does in actual life."

The only point of real difference between Breton's conception of dream and Freud's is the belief that action is catalyzed by an aspiration latent in dream, which is more an expression of Breton's desire that this be so than a consequence of reality as such, which Freud elucidated in *The Interpretation of Dreams* in such exhaustive detail that the matter could be regarded as put to bed.

If, for example, the performance of criminal activity in dream, originating in infantile desires, is more marvelous in the poetic sense than all those dark moments spanning the era of classical tragedies to the Gothic novel and roman noir, if this bloodstained aspect of dream, so close to the greatest poetic spirits such as Sade or Lautréamont, has a virtuality whose power is beyond doubt, then what sort of approach should be adopted by those of us who share with Marx the belief in the need to change the world for the better, how should we approach these dark aspects of dream, when, as Breton assumes, its tentacles genuinely incite action!

Let no one gainsay me for conflating a normative ethical position with an empirical position, that I am trying to obfuscate empirical consequences by such a normative ethical perspective. I categorically refute this. I only wish to vividly evoke what must be confronted if we are to acknowledge the power of dream to influence action.

Fortunately, the dream has remained for poetry what it was for Plato, a boon whereby even the greatest evil can exert a salutary influence, and what it was for Freud, wish fulfillment, or a kind of action in and of itself, a consummation of action, action innately capable of fulfilling our desires.

This question alone wouldn't have much practical implication if Breton's conception of dream and action as communicating vessels didn't entail a number of consequences, the present magnitude of which weighs on me at every turn.

So with dream conceived in this way, what's projected onto the screen of a future classless society in the minds of Surrealists could be conditions that such a classless society would neither be obligated nor justified to satisfy. If it is a fallacy to localize the conditions for a "liberation of the mind," as applied from the "liberation of dream," to a future classless society, then the present consequence of this error is the disillusionment among Surrealists with the evolution of Soviet reality, whose categorical fate is the fact that it is reality and has absolutely no reason to approximate the realm of dream. Freedom conceived under the sway of the "liberation of dream" cannot be of the kind that in any way might be reconciled with social reality. Through the ability to sublimate, the people of socialism have and will have no other choice but to again isolate their galvanizing asocial desires to the inspired sphere of dream and the sphere of poetry, because the design of social reality has no place for the dialectical synthesis of reality and dream, for surreality.

For that matter, reality and dream cannot be considered dialectical antitheses. Whereas reality either exists or it doesn't, whereas there is only one reality, whereas reality is all

PHOTO : V. NEZVAL

. . . where I was particularly taken with a small balcony for three suspended from a wine restaurant . . . p. 71

that does exist, dream in and of itself cannot be placed on the same conceptual scale, on the same conceptual plane, as if it were reality's antithesis, because dream is itself a product of reality, a particular form of reality-processing in the human mind.

Given Freud's view of dream as disguised fulfillment of repressed wishes — and whereas the dream owes its magical structure to the censor of consciousness, which after all announces itself during waking precisely because it acts to repress these desires — the dream will remain wholly confined to its own realm and then to those rare moments of waking life in which, because right at that moment we've ceased to be an agent of action, we become a dreaming subject, a poet.

The life-giving power of dream will be granted humanity to the extent it is allowed to become truly human, a humanity for whom the right to life will be more equitably distributed between the right to act and the right to dream. No human society (the more progressive the society, the less likely the chance) will concede that these two rights — the right to act justly, corresponding with social necessities, and the right to each dream, in which the subject would fulfill, in the dream context, repressed wishes — exist in a notional causal unity, as Breton sees it.

Let us look then at all that is entailed in resolving the reality-dream conundrum as expounded by the founder of Surrealism.

In addition to muddying the idea of a classless society by introducing a conception of freedom colored by dream, thus giving rise to disillusionment with the evolution of socialism as is, as dictated by its struggle with all manner of temporal exigencies, Breton's conception of dream and action as communicating vessels informs his attempt to create a causal connection between social emancipation and the liberation of the mind, whereby the level of the liberation of the mind is, for him, measured by how it manifests in the dream realm. If through and in socialism the mind is emancipated more from economic determinants, from property relationships in the context of private ownership and hucksters of all stripes, then a socialist system, and not even one that has reached the stage of communism, does not and will not substantially alter humanity's unconscious desires, for which the realm of dream, the realm of dreaming, will continue to be a space rigorously reserved, more rigorously even than under the brutality of an unbridled laissez-faire capitalist system.

I consider it a sign of general progress in social empathy and tastes the fact that from the era of Romanticism to our present day poets have so honed the censorship of consciousness in themselves that they scorn the dream fulfillment of their egoistical social desires, from the approbation of petty bourgeois idyllicism to the bourgeois appropriation of their mistresses; they have so honed the censorship of consciousness in themselves that in their disdain for the idyllic happiness of petty bourgeois daydreamers their deep, unconscious primal urges are fulfilled in their poetry through the method of disguise and by utilizing mechanisms analogous to those of the dream-censor.

We now come to the question of so-called waking dreams, which according to Breton's initial definition of Surrealism are "pure psychic automatism." Even though he revised his definition, albeit en passant, when he recommended in his *Second Manifesto of Surrealism* that Surrealist writers be mindful of the division between the conscious and the unconscious that arises during *écriture automatique*, from the philosophical point of view Surrealism has yet to satisfactorily clarify and precisely establish to what extent the conscious process of writing might absorb into itself aspects of the unconscious.

Here as well we might turn to Freud for guidance since it was he who discovered that unconscious wishes are able to penetrate the waking state, that our involuntary thoughts are responsible for virtually inducing a series of accidental associations, pointing to an imperative unconscious source, and a variety of faulty actions contend to fulfill our unconscious desires even during waking.

Despite Freud's irrefutable findings, this is still a long way from being able to speak of waking activities, which includes poetry, as *pure* psychic automatism. With the classics, for which an a priori rational conception of the work was an absolute requirement, it is no coincidence that irrational images distorted by the censor keeping watch over the unconscious surface only rarely.

If we take the displays of mediums, for whom poor technical training presents no obstacle to creating either paintings or written work, relatively speaking, as products of the most automatic kind, then we will surely notice the extent to which these products are rationally influenced by the naive dogmas of occultists and the extent to which they are linked, even in expression, to their own spiritualist tradition.

So when scrutinizing the automatic texts of Surrealists, the prevalence of a common quality is infallibly detected, and the rather monotonous similarities are not first and foremost the result of unconscious impulses penetrating the waking state but instead are largely the product of an analogous verbal technique, an emphasis on a similar aesthetic effect, drawing on stylistic devices borrowed from the Rimbaud-Lautréamont poetic tradition, imbued with the spirit of Apollinaire and of Dada, where the programmatic incorporation of chance has facilitated the standardization of this given style through the random combination of verbal elements.

If Surrealist automatic texts are compared with so-called Surrealist puns, or the game known as Exquisite Corpse, we find that the role played by chance is similar to poems created by pulling words out of a hat, which was the most authentic expression of Dadaism. Given these games have had an impact on the Surrealist idiom, and given their techniques were already employed by Apollinaire in his poem "The Windows," whose individual lines are created by different writers, then psychic automatism cannot be given unequivocal priority in Surrealist prose or poetry since "objective chance" plays such a crucial role in their creation, and additionally, considering how decisive for their creation is the Surrealist proclivity for a particular mode of expression, a Surrealist text or poem, these putative waking dreams, are nothing at all like night dreams either in terms of inception or in terms of structure.

While much of what defines a Surrealist text or poem is the outgrowth of a mannerism established with the help of partial psychic automatism, objective chance inherited from Dadaism, and the dictates of style, while the Surrealist genre was formed on the basis of this complex of influences, just as the fairy-tale genre, for example, is defined by an array of specific elements, then a variety of Surrealist pieties — such as the prohibition on a preconceived motif, the prohibition on meter and rhyme, the prohibition on a conscious focus on this or that effect — cannot be understood in the sense of the legitimate directives and proscriptions that come from within, that are derived from the inherent laws of the poetic process itself.

Given our knowledge of Freud's dream discoveries, that the most insignificant experience from the previous day could serve as a dream trigger, we might analogically assume that absolutely anything could serve as a poem's motif. The main question is how much dream capacity, derived from the power struggle between unconscious impulses and the censor keeping watch over the unconscious, will this motif, corresponding to the previous day's experience, be subjected to through a processing analogous to the operation of dreamwork.

If a real connection is induced between the poet's intellect and unconscious desires when creating a poem on the basis of a preconceived subject, and not, above all, on a preliminary aesthetic orientation toward a particular idiom, a particular type of image, a particular sequencing of verses, in other words, a Surrealist style, then this subject, however and for whatever reason it was conceived, even if rationally, and however and whatever its intended effect, will be transformed through the dialectical confrontation between conscious and unconscious psychic tendencies into a waking dream whose consequent form is neither a product of the subject, nor from its choice, nor from anything predetermined.

If the consequence of Surrealist mannerism and preferences is that meter and rhyme are excluded from poetry as a legitimate matter of style, then from the moment we realize that Surrealist texts are not and cannot be pure psychic automatism, the principle that holds meter and rhyme to be artificial impediments to the supposed actual functioning of thought has no applicability, and if utilized or not, their usability or non-usability, it is a matter of the relative stylistic inclinations of the poet.

Given Breton, subjectively citing Hegel, has maintained that poetry should be universal, that its translatability and therefore its potential to make a mark internationally shouldn't be encumbered with external formal impediments such as meter and rhyme, then this argument for communication with the outside also cannot claim general validity, as a great many of the most formally demanding works of poetry have found their interpreters who have succeeded in bringing them into a new language with maximal poetic authenticity. From a philosophical and psychological perspective, this argument of Breton's holds no more water than his current opinion, already proven flimsy and never adequately revised, that the expression of pure psychic automatism can be attained via the waking process.

Having succeeded in shattering the notion that Surrealist activity is an expression of pure psychic automatism, having viewed the work of poetry not as a passive reflection of the "actual functioning of thought" but as an artificial creation that in our century has extricated itself from the predominant influence of rationalism to find itself in the domain of the imagination, which blossoms in the freest and most complete way in dream, and having divested the poem of its ostensible determinacy by *pure* automatism, overestimated by Surrealism, to treat it dialectically as an aggregate of the poet's conscious and unconscious propensities, we are then able to address anew the question of poetry as directed or undirected.

If in Breton's opinion Surrealist poetry is, in the fullest sense of the word, undirected, how could he then simultaneously assert that on the one hand a Surrealist poem, undirected and resistant to any direction, might become an instrument of revolutionary activity, that is, enter the service of the Revolution, or in other words, perform the role of a conscious function, while on the other hand requiring poetry, in serving this function, to retain the power of expression it has precisely because it was engendered by pure psychic automatism!

The issue isn't merely how Breton dulls in advance the sword poetry should become by lading its functional blade with the requirement that it retain all the qualities of an undirected poem, nor is it merely how Breton underestimates poetry as a weapon at all, the issue is his, let's say, slip of the tongue when by admitting that a poem could be honed to take on an extrapoetic function he undeniably reveals that he himself doesn't consider it sacrosanct that poetry be undirected.

It follows from what I have outlined above that the poem, a product of the poet's sensibility in its entirety, directed by a poet's intellect and uninhibited obsessions, finding in the imagination and in the arcanum of dream its unforeseen marvelous, its oneiric marvelous, that the poem, this child of intention and chance, of passion and a desire for rapture, consciousness, and sleep itself, is an expression of, to the fullest extent possible, the poet's spirit, what the poet wants and knows with what is innately desired and unsuspected.

So to my mind the so-called subversive quality of Surrealist work appears to be simply an attribute of its oneirism, simply a consequence of imaginatively fulfilling taboo unconscious human desires, which are as discontinuous from the realm of action as is the guardian of sleep and executor of repressed unconscious desires, the dream.

A malign dream that is a social good because the dream is gratified by the *dreaming* of evil, which is rightly excluded from the sphere of action, goes hand in hand with good in the most poignant way we have ever known in the work of Lautréamont — in *Les Chants de Maldoror* dialectical good in the thrall of a dream of evil and in *Poésies* the codification of good in the conscious sense — and what this work of works accomplishes in both its monumental and seemingly incongruous parts is a grand integration of the poet's mental state. If in *Maldoror* one is denuded of unconscious desires, which are fulfilled through a sovereign catharsis that is an end in itself, in *Poésies* one is placed in opposition to emotional megalomania and the negativism of Romantic conceptions of humankind in the service of hope, in the service of good, to the limits of human necessity.

For that matter, compared to all other poetry *Maldoror* is unrivaled in its fantastic balance between its intentional design, which is an attack on both the man and the creator in the name of good vs. evil as directed by the poet's conscious obsessions, and its oneiric aspect, nonpredetermined and gushing out during the very process of creation from under the pen of the person writing. Even though, "A man or a stone or a tree is about to begin the fourth canto" of *Maldoror*, it begins face to face with Isidore Ducasse, who never lets his mind wander even for a moment from what his song is and should be.

While the incomparable magnificence of *Maldoror* is inherent in the utterly active approach taken by Lautréamont for its composition, with conscious forethought of its ultimate meaning and impact, the marvel of *Maldoror* is in its dialectical fusion of his primary approach, this forethought, with the unsuspected insights of oneirism, which were left to develop within him as freely as possible. Compared to Lautréamont's great dialectical synthesis of consciously intended frames of mind with elements of the unconscious, many works of Surrealism, even Rimbaud's *Illuminations*, appear to be merely impressive — and this is because both *Illuminations* and Surrealist poetry to a large extent lack that one facet that is, as we can see, indispensable for greatness : conscious direction.

In light of my recent view that to date there's been a dichotomy between poetry for its own sake and poetry in the service of social change, that poetry qua poetry and poetry as a weapon are mutually exclusive, I have come to the opinion that the former is undirected and incapable of being directed, while the latter requires an objective, a position, which this reasoning contradicts, so that from now on the form constructed will not hinge on poetry (is it to blame for reproducing so often through mitosis?) but on poets and to what extent they manage to unify what manifests from a conscious approach and from the oneiric arising out of the contest between unconscious desires and the censor watching over them.

Lautréamont is such a marvelous example also because he lights our way today more than at any other time. No other society will have such an ardent and tangible appreciation for the aspirations he demonstrated in *Poésies* as one that is built on hope and good, a socialist society. If Lautréamont was wholly justified in rebuking the poseurs among the greatest poets of the past and of his era, while at the same time he inimitably towered over their faculties of imagination in terms of the power of oneirism, then more than anyone else it is in his footsteps, as revealed as well as occluded by Surrealists, that we are called to follow, to seek out a great dialectical synthesis of good in the service of life and the repressed malice of dream, between the benefits of a conscious poetic approach and the benefits of the incalculable potential of oneirism.

The scintillating experience gained by Surrealism on the fertile ground of oneirism, thanks to André Breton's initiative for its magic, to Paul Eluard for its simplicity, to Max Ernst for the discovery of collage, to Dalí for his attempts to introduce active thought into a receptive technique for pursuing associations and for the whole of his experimental activity to reveal the emotional charge of objectivity, these experiences in the oneiric realm reaped by Surrealism will remain, even beyond the mistakes that have been spawned in the womb of Surrealist thought (which I have tried to rectify here) the greatest thing ever done in our century for poetry, for its glorious renaissance.

Although I reproach Surrealism for some of its mistakes

from a position I have inevitably arrived at with each passing day, it is not, nor desires to be, the critique of someone who observes from the distance of the opposite shore, but rather a form of self-criticism addressed to the man who more than anyone has earned my respect and has had more courage than anyone else to seek (and in that case why not errantly?), that is, André Breton.

I see him emerging from the train at Prague's Wilson Station before the cameras of those who have been infected by my affection for him. Emotionally I see his head drifting down the narrow lanes behind Týn Church, I see his eyes turn for the first time to the white gulls over the river immersed in night and flowing along the ghostly silhouettes of the terraced buildings up to its crown of Prague Castle.

I see him ecstatically bend over the St. Vitus agates. I see his eyes blaze when I guide them for the first time to those affecting surrealistic folk objects that are Prague house signs. I see his eyes wander along the roofs of the Ungelt and blaze in the vaulted wine bar with a view of Old Town's astronomical clock. I see his affable smile with which he received my enthusiasm unconditionally. I see his anxiously pensive eyes disappear in the window of the train as it pulls away from the Prague of our dreams.

What I would give for this hastily sketched corrective of certain Surrealist principles to have been written by him, if I could've summoned his fading image from Mexico to be here at this table, to find the right words, the right tone, that would endow this corrective, which my most vibrant conscience has compelled me to write, with the same ardor I had when clasping his hand.

For if Surrealism, despite the errors I believe contained in some of its formulations, is able to give me that blistering vertigo, that extended enchantment, that daybreak to which I gladly awake from my nocturnal dreams as to a day offering the prospect of even greater radiance, I do not consider myself, nor should I be considered, one of those apostates who sobered up by parting ways with the Surrealist Group.

On the contrary, my love for the revelations of Surrealism, so poignantly dovetailing with my own dreams, a perfect correspondence with them, has persuaded me to write these lines. And if it were possible to reciprocate something that has awakened in us the most luminous, most joyful enchantment, then it would be with this, if I am not mistaken, that we attempt to keep at bay from our beloved thoughts all the pitfalls that enter our field of vision.

Mood lighter, I return to the winding stairs down which Prague leads me. For as the daily droning of the bombers flying overhead has made clear, there is no time, time flies by and tomorrow might be too late. Our covenant with life is not forever, and your last testament cannot be put off indefinitely when confronted daily with the growing urgency to say everything, to say it all in a single sentence, to say more than ever needed to be said at any other time, to ask your steps with increasing anxiety where they are taking you, where they would like to take you, where they would rather not go at the cost of life, at the cost of death.

The poet is someone who destroys and creates myths, who destroys them to create new ones, always more real.

And a great new realism, its path having been cleared by Surrealism, is coming — it is on the way, it is being born.

There is no more breathtaking view of the spectacle of life (if at the moment we are not being brutally assailed by a grand persecutor, which social life is, and exposed to the plethora of tribulations with which nature itself hounds us) than from the balcony of a café shaded by a red and yellow striped awning — and retracted just enough to offer us a glimpse of the magical perspective that begins with the Petřín Lookout Tower, continues through the two towers of the Strahov Monastery to Hradčany, above and under which the sun is setting on the surface of the Vltava, and ends in a complex of three buildings attached to Charles Bridge that form a narrow sight-hole at Karlovy lázně into and out of which trams roll at regular intervals.

The many diverse and unexpectedly connected details that make up our dream are impossible to count. The details fade, and the spectator is left with a feeling that life is worth living.

It's hard to say what a whitewashed building edging the water means to any of the customers on the terrace, such a small urban structure that could just as well be an old mill of the kind found on a farm.

Another building, entirely set apart and submerged in thick foliage, is a two-story ark in which one would gladly spend the summer. Two or three fishermen, more like the recollection of a Dutch painting than verisimilitude hunched over a long rod, come here in place of a rural song to mediate contact between our childhood and the Middle Ages, whose denizens are marching across Charles Bridge straight toward us. Yes, the statues are walking, on the move, in motion because Charles Bridge is not bereft of walkers. Yet as soon as we step onto the bridge ourselves, this wonder ceases. If we choose, we're in a theater. I don't know why, maybe the river's magical presence wishes that out of all those little street theaters our attention gravitates toward the one whose centerpiece is a man bearing an infant on his shoulder.

He is Christophorus carrying the Christ Child across the river. Legend has it that the child was heavy as lead. I like this legend. I like it mostly because poetry, too, is this type of conveyor of the small and light that with each step sink our feet deeper and deeper into the earth, until we are suddenly sunk up to our knees, as if crossing a bog.

And then suddenly buried up to the neck our frantic heads shout and shout and fly off to where the laws of gravity no longer apply. This light we have borne, which all at once has flung us somewhere unknown, tells our head, floating along a window from out of nowhere, its name. This name is our uncanny double who lacks the ability to feel pain, this name is Lucifer.

I must confide to you the circumstances under which I met this Lucifer one day. As we say : It was pouring down.

You know the Prague rain. But this time it had transformed all of Old Town into the rattling of glass drops that carried off a lady's shoe as a greeting to those who crave to kiss a woman's foot and place a dusty cheek on her knee.

I think lightning flashed a few times (maybe only once) — I took fright. And truly, before my eyes floated a shoe.

I would say the girl who lost it was no more than seventeen. I could be wrong, of course, and she was a widow.

I forgot to add that we're on the edge of Josefovská Street, just a few steps from Pařížská Avenue.

Today that spectacular convergence of straight lines (not quite meeting, but the presence of eternity here is different, sweeter, in the form of a belated mail truck that fails to reach its destination and instead begins to sell off its contents to passersby) did not afford the view I so love, the view of the Letná Hill treetops. And how could it when one person was dueling with the next with water swords created by the funnels of rain.

The shoe drifted past. If I were to say that I looked around for the unfortunate owner of this indispensable and alluring object, I wouldn't be telling the truth. Not that I would be lying either, because I did look around, but only like someone who wanted to take possession of something that didn't belong to him.

The creaking of doorposts could hardly startle us more than this evening's specious curtains that formed barely one-square-meter closets around the impassioned onlooker. Put plainly, I wanted to grab that lady's pump as if my soul's salvation depended on it.

Stealing an object of desire is no simple matter. This is borne out by crime statistics and the cheerful smiles of those serving time for petty theft, hardly worth an attorney's time, next to those who have secure lodgings behind bars for a period longer than puberty.

In other words, I was indecisive.

I am well aware that a police station is a mere twenty paces away. I noticed it one early morning when three guardians of public order were trying to prevent a woman from stripping naked. What was she thinking, in front of a police station! No idea. The laws of the soul are as varied as the laws governing falling leaves, but the point is that I knew of this inhospitable den's existence, where justice would've been meted out to me like the candelabraed rain. I hardly had any reason to be afraid! Neither cops nor their quarry have much use for such foul weather. We all love peace and quiet.

I refuse to feel any shame for relating how utterly captivated I was by this floating object. It was something strangely habitable — then again — while still in the cradle mystery had cast before my eyes a golden fly, and I've regularly had to shoo it off my sleeve ever since. Maybe I desired to meet an attractive woman at that moment. (Such a shoe appearing in such an unusual circumstance guarantees that its wearer is conversant with beauty.)

I now meant to bend down, with every intention to place myself entirely at the mercy and mercilessness of the succulent drops from which I had been sufficiently sheltered in the vestibule of a nearby tavern. I now mentally said farewell to the neatness of my shirt. Yet when I took the first step toward my objective, which I was ready to seize without hesitation and without any scruples (such as they are called), when I had overcome the initial surge of slipping along the pool of water lubed with some kind of glossy black oil, I was halted by something coming from the side, as if out of the void, from the side of the marvelous, now assuming an especially bizarre mien.

At the midpoint of this cylinder intersected by the wind to form a kind of double funnel, in the middle of this gigantic hourglass of rain brilliantly illuminated by a light pendulating a short distance away, a ridiculous little man appeared whom I do not intend to describe. I didn't see his face. Besides, it's enough to tell you he was hunchbacked. He was hunchbacked like the distance of two spools in a loom prematurely put into motion by a man unacquainted with how recondite this rather socially bleak profession, or like two roosters locked in an embrace, one of which was driving its beak into a discarded pipe stem, unclear whose, or like three barrels whose contents could not be measured having recently become subject to the law on material leakage. He was hunchbacked. This did not mean he wasn't young. I could also compare him to an acrobat walking a slack rope with enviable confidence, considering the dexterity he displayed when snatching the forbidden object.

Then I heard a scream. Before this scream could help me figure out what was going on (don't believe for a second I wasn't curious about what might unfold!) and discover from whose throat, or at least open mouth, it had issued, I saw two little fists no larger than an aspergillum (a gem might have been hanging from the wrist, or it could have been the rain that provided the ornament) pounding with such force on the humped back of the man, whom at this moment I considered my rival, that he shrunk as if he were being hammered into the ground.

I heard a whole litany of colorful epithets, which some might have taken as heinous abuse if not coming (now there wasn't the slightest doubt) from the mouth of a woman who gave every indication of being quite pretty.

If my assumption was correct, then this woman had likely returned home to be confronted by a strange man who had the misfortune of being a hunchback. Maybe this insidious shadow had even removed her shoe to persuade her to do something she evidently did not want to do. I don't know. Besides, I am here to report what I saw as a random (and invisible) party to the event, the meaning of which escapes me. I thought I saw the shrinking man laugh. I am sure of it. He laughed like a goat, because no other creature has a laugh like a hyperbolic oboe.

At that point I saw the profile of the woman who was resolved to win her street battle by employing tactics generally considered beyond the pale. She was indeed beautiful. As beautiful as the moon, if I were to be more specific.

I would say she was choking the man, to whom I had absolutely no interest in being introduced. I would say she was choking him, if the neck can be choked by such an inapt instrument as the knees of a lovely woman. That is to say, she straddled him with the loveliest part of her body, lashed by the downpour, seated as if in a saddle on the neck of the bleating creature.

All of this happened in an interval shorter than a magnesium flash that allows the contours of objects veiled by darkness to penetrate the sensitive emulsion of a photographic plate. This runt carried her off, whooping it up to boot! He carried her off like an old warped beam carrying white light.

• • •

I don't know why I recalled this scene without sequel when today, having been lured by the floodlights illuminating Charles Bridge, I lingered longer than usual before the statue of St. Christopher.

If you walk from Old Town Square toward the Municipal Library, and at dusk when the square on U Radnice Street is deserted, you will come across a little pub called the Green Frog, whose very location between a junk shop and the stone wall of a building that remembers the skies of bygone centuries, along with its inner garden, makes it one of the most magical refuges for couples who yearn for the tenebrous, as well as for the poetic soul driven by a persecution mania to places bereft of witnesses.

If it's a sweltering day, which I bring up because such days lend Prague her little known yet most wondrous southern qualities, and on this little square squats a still air, which I know from the quiet corners of Paris and the old Italian parts of Nice, I am rewarded by a rare spectacle that has kept me returning here for some time.

It's not just the proximity of Platnéřská Street, where the Iron Knight sleeps, to awaken only once a century, a street I deeply love, which projects toward the Green Frog one of its bleakest structures, a six-floor edifice with an official seal on its façade, it is the rather mysteriously intricate perspective down Kaprová Street and the short, deep perspective down Maiselova Street, and then that junk shop, its brickwork painted red, and the house from 1664, and ultimately even that dreary New City Hall building and the stench, but more than anything it's the secretiveness of this little square, which could be the center of any number of old towns, and then a kind of ineffable nostalgia that makes this spot so dear to me.

Here I feel genuinely far from everything that could remind me of the people and things to which I am bound by obligation. Here I am truly abroad.

I was quite moved when one of my closest friends, who doesn't live in Prague and whom I acquainted with this watering hole, told me that every time he visits now he makes it a point to stop by the Green Frog.

After all, only when he said this did the name of this drinking den of scant luxury hit me and lead me to look above its entrance, where I was elated to see one of those house signs that represent for me a key to the complex beauty of Prague : the relief of a green frog crawling head first down the wall.

I was also happily aware that King Václav IV, the only king for whom I have any affinity, used to visit this tavern and that as a sign of their contempt for his memory the king's enemies bestowed this establishment on a man befitting a character in my next Gothic novel, the executioner Jan Mydlář.

And this little square, whose charm I vainly try to conjure, has retained its magic for one additional reason : no trams run here — and when a bus or automobile should happen to drive by, it only creates the impression of a quaint anachronism of the kind so appealing to collagists.

While making my rounds through Prague only rarely would I encounter a familiar face at any of the places I enjoyed frequenting, such as the Green Frog, or the patio in front of Malostranská Café, which reveals to us behind that inauspicious monument to Ernest Denis, so cumbersomely placed amid fairy-tale airiness, one of the more astounding concordances to be found on Malostranské Square.

The knight who slept for several centuries once appeared

to me here, and I cannot reach his palace. Today, having tested the relative resistance of this square to mundanity, I make no demands on my imagination when I am in its midst. The simple fact is that when I'm sitting in such spots not a single familiar face has yet to remind me that I am not in an illustration. The sensation that usually overcomes me is the same as I experienced many times in childhood when I would see Prague in a peephole diorama, the same detachment and dissociation from my surroundings, the same inaccessibility, the same dreamlike peculiarity that I felt in the classroom then.

I really do not understand those Prague poets who are satisfied to congregate in maybe only two or three cafés the whole year. My wish for them would be that one day they approach Prague like a stranger. Such is how I walk through the city, how I've walked through her for several years.

I have never run into one these poets on Žitná Street, for instance, which resembles a moving van barreling down the road. Because of the street's incredible clamor, its unbelievable bustle, I find here more than anywhere else objects of daily use in the most fantastical situations. I'm more than happy to surrender to the street's ragtag hubbuby sidewalk charm, a sidewalk partly occupied by the Paris Café giving onto the Baroque rectory standing on the corner of Žitná and Štěpánská streets. Nowhere else will you find more shops than here. I especially love this street on a weekday, and enjoy peering through its nocturnal vista toward Karlova Square, especially if a fair is being held with stalls selling Turkish delight. And I will never forget the strangeness of this nighttime Prague, as if out of nowhere, when I lean over it across the railing enclosing the yard of St. Stephen's Church. I like to stop here at night at a bookstore where a glittering crystal ball lay on a black tray. I never think about it during the day, but at night I have to satisfy my desire to possess it and place it above my books.

After all, from here it's just a short walk to one of the quietest spots in all of Prague — Karlov, behind whose church (legend has it that the architect had help from the devil to construct its vaulted ceiling) is a park where you'll forget what century you're in. Once I was sitting there as evening fell and nearly took fright at the sight of an airplane circling overhead. I wondered what it was doing there. It didn't belong. And when it had flown past the field of vision of the vaulting towering over the park, where you feel more alone than those places you travel to in summer to find solitude, there was no reason to give it any more thought. My gaze slid from it to a slice of eternity whose adopted form captured my attention : a bed of red poppies.

I know only a single place where I have felt over my many years living in Prague so boundlessly disengaged from the city's overall rhythm, so infinitely distant from all those paths taken out of obligation — and this place is the old Prague Conservatory from the period when it was located in a corner of the quad at the Emmaus Monastery.

Talent notwithstanding, I liked going into this courtyard to listen to the hum of musical instruments, the sounds clearly audible, sounds colliding, the sounds of tuning. It's the same as when in the depths of the garden or on some craggy spot in the schoolyard I would happily listen to my father at the piano as he taught my sister how to play études. Those études, just like the fragmented cadences of the piano, violin, or oboe, exerted a special power over my heart precisely because they were so nakedly disjointed. They imposed no melody on me. In my mind I was back in those sweet apprentice years of long ago, so fondly recalled because they have passed, all the stress from the fact that as children we are required to learn having dissipated. And I imagined I was holding in my hand one of the loveliest brochures I have ever seen, with the pictures of musical instruments. Vibrating in my memory as well was a now very yellowed price list of the *Collection Litolff* with its alphabetical index of opera composers whom I so wished to meet. And the quad of the Emmaus Monastery moreover was mobbed by sparrows.

Lest you think I am just stringing you along with charms (perhaps you'll agree that what has the power to move me are greater or lesser charms) that are not "unique to Prague," that we could find anywhere else if we were so inclined, I confess to the thrill it gives me when I chance upon them in Prague. Maybe sounds such as those floating around the old Emmaus conservatory wouldn't have so utterly convulsed my soul if I hadn't encountered them in the very quad of that monastery. For nothing that commands our interest, the degree of which, great or small, corroborates the degree of our happiness, would have existed, would have lived its singular existence, if it had not been placed in certain contexts and not in others, in situations one way or another discrete. I maintain that

PHOTO : V. NEZVAL

. . . and that as a sign of their contempt for his memory the king's enemies bestowed this establishment on a man befitting a character in my next Gothic novel, the executioner Jan Mydlář . . . p. 95

the magic of certain spontaneously intoxicating situations directly correlates to the fact that Prague was where I experienced them.

I've always had a pep in my step when walking down Provaznická Street since the time magazines devoted ink to the news that the corpse of a man murdered by his own daughter had been discovered there concealed in a chimney. In eras when the human imagination was more adept at creating legends than it is today, this house would unavoidably have been seen as one of the spookiest. And isn't the poet just that member of the human race who should ensure that old Prague legends remain alive today? Rather than meeting contemporary writers in places whose stimulating atmosphere I often fail to understand, I encounter the shades of the former custodians of what today is now legend. I often sit for whole hours in their presence and listen to their voice.

This voice, which does not intrude on my most intimate dreams, imparted something to me that now has only a nebulous connection to the memory of who was doing the telling. Though I learn no tangible details, yet I am rapt, stirred. This voice, drowned out by the din of autos, the clacking of hooves, and noises whose source cannot be traced, cannot be guessed, this voice, which many might mistake for the wind, or for twilight, this voice is dear to me.

This is how we are spoken to every so often by some old tome we hungrily reach for in a decrepit bookshop we have decided to enter. Our desire to have it is often thwarted by some other design. And if we do take it home, we won't read it. Divested of the wondrous atmosphere in which it was found, it loses its eloquence, no longer beguiles, its mysteriousness wanes. And yet what is has given us will never be taken away, never completely sink into oblivion. And neither will the voice of invisible witnesses to ages from which hardly any legends remain, coming to me as I wander the out-of-the-way parts of Old Town, Malá Strana, Hradčany, or Josefov. I know this voice chooses me as its medium when I least expect it. I want nothing other for this book, cannot want anything more, than to let it murmur over the blackened roofs or in the overcoats of forlorn secondhand shops that don't see a single customer all day long. This voice has the quality of being able to call out its, *Here I am*, and then fade into an indistinct murmur; this voice is able to manifest itself between the time on my pocket watch, always running ahead, and the time on the clock looming over the Old-New Synagogue, whose hands run backward. Its presence resembles a still silence that wouldn't be so harrowing if it weren't accentuated now and again by the honks of car horns punctuating the air before immediately fading.

At this point I would like to say a word about the Prague of Rabbi Loew, about her spellbound nostalgia that every so often possesses the power (especially on those days when storm clouds gather in the sky without a storm ever arriving) to leave its confines, whose remnants lie in the Jewish ghetto, and fly off to all the city's quarters as a wing too long outspread for flight in some old museum.

Rabbi Loew's *shem* is placed under the tongue of all things here, under the tongue as well of the walker who after all is formed of the same type of stone that covers all of Prague. All that is required for me to evoke the profound enchantment I feel here with each step I take is to recall an incident that occurred on a visit to the Jewish Museum in April 1935 in the company of Paul Eluard.

After we had signed the guest book, displayed there for that purpose and revealed to us by a puppet-like young Jewish man, gesturing awkwardly, whom we took to be a deaf mute, as we browsed the Museum's wonderful flotsam, our guide made no effort to show us around, unlike those at the Cemetery and the Old-New Synagogue, nor offer us a single word of commentary (confirming our impression that he was mute, or, may he forgive us . . .), and when it seemed we were out of earshot of all but the centuries-old walls, this boy, whom we'd already forgotten, said in a high falsetto something I will never forget : *Surrealists*.

What does it matter if we discovered later who this curious young man was, where he could have known us from, what does the eventual explanation of this miracle matter, an explanation actually very simple and by no means surprising to those of us who do not know and have never known anything about miracles in the metaphysical sense — despite this explanation, the miracle stayed a miracle in the poetic sense, because even before it could be explained, it ignited in us, no matter how brief a moment in space, time, and causation, an eternal flame, so that as we were leaving the old Jewish Quarter in the direction of Old Town Square, all three of us were certain that this person we had just met was Isaac Laquedem, who joined Guillaume Apollinaire as he made the rounds of Prague's dives, whom Apollinaire saw collapse on the street, and for whom an old Jew rent his garment.

I wrote the poem “Ragman” in 1927 under the sway of those selfsame eerie shudders I nearly always feel when my steps involuntarily carry me toward Maiselova Street (where I enjoy walking — maybe because in such Prague locales I’ve never sensed the feeble voice of the banal), which were revived when recalling the scene that took place at the Jewish Museum. I believe the poem will give you some idea of my enchantment with the Fifth District, that is, Josefov, and allow me to accompany you through it, almost wordless, in that profound silence that lay over everything : the walls, the squalid little shops, and especially the deeply ecstatic faces of old junk dealers standing before their shopfronts as if performing in some otherworldly drama.

How different the neighborhoods in the rain
and windows with tattered curtains
It’s raining on cabmen’s lamps
and on night owls in sodden districts

A ragpicker
execrates Saint Teresa
says she was a Neapolitan
during the War of the Roses

Yet he lightly teeters
between blossoms of gray brandy
and his shoes ravage memory
on the carpet of twenty years

The stench of fates tussle
on his back
whose hump clambers
up the chambermaid's shift

In times of carnations
her crossed legs
guarded dreams
whose cobweb frays under fingers on lace hems

Bric-a-brac
caught in the act
in his aged wheezing
attempts one last pimpish blush

But the ragpicker his neck tingling
with the soaked blue of that vanished virginity
curses another Christian woman
crushing lice with jerking shoulder blades

How beautiful these small Jews
returning to ancient quarters with their purchases
where rain falls for their sake
while on first floors one street over is a starlit night

A vindictive innocence in their thoughts
and tender festival feasts in their knots
they listen with bated breath
to scraps of melodies from belated musicians

A witness to Beethoven's sonatas
the skirts his eyes rested on during long walks
as if exposing themselves to his glory
waiting for a liberator

Naked camisoles without halters
flaccid astral bodies abandoned by their angels
and grimy under twenty- thirty-year dust
yet with the tenderness of Communion knees

Mourning bodices
where vestiges of young widows' white breasts
are firm despite the plissé of time
sobbing when knocked against the corset

The rusted buttons of evening gowns
still sob even now under fingernails
on sofas in the light of a street
that diverts words from risible intents

But so too the battered shoes of poets
the fluttering of cotillion curtains
altar bedsheets and those blue
masks kissed in the dark

The ragman's whole trove
exciting him not a whit
makes me love these precincts
of rainy nights and stuffed night owls

I lift my eyes above the rooftops
to the hoary heavens of these relics
and on any star encounter
the nostalgic eyes of women passed

The onset of winter
and Manon Lescaut waits for a carriage
at the Opera where she has just been taken by an old marquis
whose cravat strangles the ragman

How different the streets without walkers
and windows through which stars fly into mirrors
while tenants immersed in sleep
enter novels lying shut on nightstands

And the otiose poet sleeps standing
as he counts off all the names of women
as if playing a guitar
with his ragman's bundle

This denizen of the streets
propped up by a gate corner
sleeps on the soft pillow of his burden
and rattles imaginary keys

and execrates Saint Poetry
says she was a Neapolitan
yet the hour is late and rain falls on cabmen's lamps
and on brandy blossoms in sodden districts

Tell me, eye, open over a white sheet of paper when I'd barely started to write this book, tell me, eye, whose color changes according to where we're walking at the moment, according to how large or small the piece of sky hoisted above narrow gondolas, into which we gladly stray, but according, too, to the color of my eyes when riveted on you, tell me, eye, that you saw all those traces in the dust of the city's cobblestones that for us will constitute Prague when these lines have reached their end.

Tell it to me, or don't. Better to say nothing. You know what it is to silently stare at an obdurately intrusive wall that has claimed the right, for reasons seldom fully understood (because we seldom pause, and even when we do, still we continue to walk, without endpoint), to mesmerize us as if writing were suddenly to appear on it, or at least a sketch, if not our complete picture. You know what this is, as do I.

Is not the poetic soul always somewhat like the outcast to whom all doors are locked by seven turns of the key? What others look for behind tightly drawn curtains, we have sought almost exclusively in the streets and in the passageways as if we feared that stopping anywhere for longer than it takes to get supremely drunk would cause our ossification. Besides, it's better this way. It's better not to get used to the coffin too soon, even if it's equipped with the most modern amenities civilization has to offer. It's better this way. At least let's leave no door open anywhere, and thieves will present less a danger than the distant whizz of locusts. And may these lines conclude a hundred times over, the city of steel will always open its gates to us with the coming of a new autumn.

My gait is that of a rustic when surveying his fields, from

place to place, from street to street, to examine the height of the vermilion weeds of dream. You have seen, eye, of what types of metamorphoses this wild plant is capable. And no one, absolutely no one, will be able to extirpate this miracle weed, not the wiles of life, not the misery of duty, not the heavy boots of cruel whim, no one and nothing. Yet I do think for some matters it is wiser to say nothing. For any contemplation of love suffers from the artificial process of drainage, the science of which civil engineering has mastered so well. Timorous or highly condensed souls anguish over such verbal sophistry and would prefer that a face not blush so often. It's better not to bother with all this pretense and leave it for the less passionate among us. Besides, I never wanted an entourage nipping at my heels. And those who become bewitched by the spell we are tailoring for life, their eyes will no longer have to pry. We have no problem greeting them, or, we will not acknowledge one another's presence. Are not the most profound strophes of a poem, which keep us in their thrall, always holding us captive, composed for us by the capricious shift of a leg and not by a fountain pen? They are. So do not be too troubled, beautiful eye, as you observe how rapidly this book approaches its end. After all, it is nothing more than a brief extract from a fascicle without end. Just smile, beautiful eye! Just smile under your lid, even though you don't know, even though I don't know, that it continues to flutter as if each second were a coming into life and leaving it. And the word "end," which fills us with such dread, is likewise just the twitch of an eyelid, simultaneously implying a beginning. Farewell, eye, from which a white period floats down onto this line!

A little girl slinks along the viaduct below the Vyšehrad cliff. Her lessons tucked under her left arm, her right hand crumbling a bread roll like someone about to feed the fish. Not a soul anywhere for her to alarm. A bell peals somewhere in a nearby house embedded into the cliff. Maybe this, too, is just an illusion. No one would believe me if I said it was February. The noonday water glimmers and roils as if seven-hundred cackling peacocks were in it, on such a sunny day.

What a well-behaved girl! Her right hand chastely holds onto her skirt as if something would spill onto the ground from her lap. Rather than a lap, let's think of it as a supple, slightly hazy mirror basking in the sunshine. Such a dear girl! You could say she was allowed to leave school early because it's her birthday — and now she's traipsing about, looking for the first daisy.

Splash!

Everyone was at a loss to explain how it could have happened so fast. Such a small girl and such a high railing! So high and cold that a steaming pink child's hand would freeze onto it. How did it happen! No one knows. No one knows if she set down her schoolwork, so meticulously organized, on the ground with the bend of the knee and gentle squat girls are taught. No one knows why she buttoned up her coat collar like someone readying to go out into a stormy day. No one knows if she pulled the beret over her golden curls with both hands, or as if mechanically running a comb through them. And the main thing no one knows is which angel, in the form of lightness, lifted and carried both her little legs (I believe it was both at once!) across that iron balustrade above the steep bank. She was, after all, no marionette pulled higher by a string in the hand of an invisible Ares! Simply out of the question.

The ineluctable law of gravity forces us to recognize the water parting under her at virtually the same instant it closes over her.

Before even a minute had passed it was over, and not a single scream. Something had happened no one would wish for. From the direction of the cabins of Podolí, having emerged at the last moment at a bend in the river, Aquarius walked along the embankment. His steely eyes fixed on the surface, on the glint of the maiden's head. The vessel in his hand assumed a calm position on the waterfront walkway, and Aquarius dove headfirst into the waves. It would be remiss not to note that at the moment he rolled up his shirt sleeves, his hand signaled to three carts approaching with their cargoes of coal.

A shame they weren't sacks of flour majestically moving at the leisurely pace of a wagon wending its way to Prague's mills. The contrast wouldn't have been so stark to the passersby who had begun to suddenly congregate when they trained their eyes on the gleaming black mass of coal bearing a huge white bouquet bordered in gold and tied down with ropes, while above this load fluttered sheets of paper like flecks of snow.

To complete a book! There are books whose conclusion is the end of the story, no matter if a good or bad ending, a story more or less radiant, its life sketched by this or that dream, a life we hold in our hands.

But you, soul, who delights in cataclysms, like roses faded

PHOTO : V. NEZVAL

. . . this voice is able to manifest itself between the time on my pocket watch, always running ahead, and the time on the clock looming over the Old-New Synagogue, whose hands run backward . . . p. 101

or freshly dispersed in windows without end (if night is falling on the city, you hear the quiet, anxious approach of a wolf who plaintively lays its head, buried in stars, on a giant rosebud and howls like shutters falling closed behind a thief), in windows where I appear with a lantern in my hand so that I can look upon Prague, turning from side to side and accepting or refusing the summer tremors, you, soul, now being lit by the red afterglow of the sun, pausing on its perambulation over the forest where the clamor of Prague is now hushed, you, soul, know that this book is nothing more and nothing less than an open cage (the canary of morning, large as three-hundred vegetable carts clustering in the wee hours at Masaryk Station, abandons its wirework home to alight on my or your head and warble a long litany of rebukes at the author who has guided us in fits and starts and who knows that the final page of his book is a door he will go through tomorrow or the day after, unless the jesters of *La Carnaval de Nice* see fit to drag him by the coattails into a recess whose historical torture implements frighten him not a bit!).

Put differently, there are genres in which we are just slightly more animated puppets, tethered by a hair to our reason, which tugs at us while the ground under our free and so determined steps hurtles past like the first railway, whose construction was based on the landaus that have disappeared for good from Prague's squares.

Better put, an author who like someone afflicted with a toothache or paranoia, chained to his life, runs through a city he would like to crown so that above it (until he dies and his future work makes him more interesting to the world than his quite ruddy face) the most sublime condors of the human race might rendezvous and weave from its fibers, a scattershot of zigzags, tapestries of triumphal or (even better) hyperrealistic verse.

As soon as these lines, spinning like a fan between the room of my brain readied for moving and a storm gathering over the Rieger Gardens to deliver Prague a refreshing wallop, have left my pen (whose thinking is just as guarded as sparrows now flying low around the trumpets filling a Sunday with their wind, now high like the folk wisdom of those who have learned to divine the weather from the flight of these adroit scissors) I will set off several more times with the speed of thought ignited on all sides by an agony that will allow me at least on these final pages to include what I have grossly neglected, to unleash a dash of lightning before the leaden period drops after the words *the end*.

While we are not always the masters of situations requiring us to pack our bags (even if the approximate date of departure was given or chosen in advance), the patience of readers should never be abused, and while it is incumbent that we conclude at one of the given means of how we measure (it could be early morning, when the first passenger-less tram rumbling out of the terminal crows under my window overlooking Král Jiří Square, or it could be on the day when it's abundantly clear that I will be leaving Prague for an unknown number of weeks, if it is not the arcane law governing the composition of poetry collections), I reserve the right to excise with scissors the size of medieval swords the parts of these pages I might like to include in other books of mine — in other words, I am ready to bring *A Prague Flâneur* to a close.

Like someone visiting a slew of shops with sofas, pianos, and frames to furnish an apartment for either himself or someone he is attached to by one of those bonds that is his destiny as a human being, I had to travel hundreds of kilometers on foot and thousands of kilometers in spirit until I was able to furnish the Prague before my eyes, until I made her into the type of dwelling that conformed to my tastes, until I outfitted her in such a way that when I returned I wouldn't have the unwanted feeling of someone reliant on generic lodgings, and so that those by my side (no need for us ever to meet) who will share the haunts of this city, which Princess Libuše envisioned at a time its existence was far more inchoate than on the day I first came speeding toward her on a train, will not feel they've been invited to a city under a cloud of smoke.

If the brief explanation I have just given makes me a latter-day workman for Charles IV, one of his builders endowed with a brain inflamed by an insatiable desire for beauty, to raise over the timeless towers, coming from an age when the human spirit preferred to give substance to its ideas through a passion for building, several seductive voices that would attempt with the very best of intentions to enrich life and to test as benignly as possible the power of suggestion, then I maintain that I have succeeded in establishing a connection between some of Prague's arcana and the human spirit.

One time when I visited the cemetery at Vyšehrad, whose uncommon location on the cliff on which one of the most illustrious histories sits like a log, I was happy that I could forgo the obligatory sorrow (to which I'm particularly susceptible, just like anyone who unquestionably loves someone in this world more than oneself) and immerse myself in the expansive waves of the creative effervescence (thereby dispelling any thoughts of death) of those poetic spirits who've been buried here longer than the mourning of the bereaved.

After leaving the cemetery, I popped into the National Café that very same evening, and if my spirits were lifted by a ship when I glanced at the wood paneling covering the walls, it was a pledge from fate that I was called to say more about this city than to merely act as tour guide to her notable landmarks.

To the one who hasn't shrunk from reading my work this far, my advice is that one day when having a meal of stewed kidneys, which famished and impatient he helped to prepare, and eating this meal under the kitchen lamp or in the room where between bites his eyes can roam over the spines of books in his personal library, he should defy habit and throw a cloak over his shoulders and traverse the Castle courtyards with his eyes shut, and when the astronomical clock chimes ten-fifteen, walk through these deserted courtyards three times while holding a glowing cigarette to the sky until his head bends low to track the length of St. Vitus Cathedral from the bottom up to the highest point.

Then he should resist the thirst he feels and stand a moment before Vikárka Restaurant (if he wants to hear the sound of chatter from bygone centuries) and pretend he lost a ring in nearby Golden Lane and has come here to look for it.

If this wasn't cause enough to be ecstatic this day, a feeling I know well and subsist on as if it were extra mature cheese, he should stand before the Archbishop's Palace like that fellow who came from Italy as the bastard child of someone who needed to be spared the slings and arrows of public outrage, like a bastard child accustomed to the bustle of a port who is suddenly swept away by a blizzard before Christmastime.

Under the arcade bordering one side of Loretánské Square, let him then be addressed by a woman who afterward will admit it would be better to disappear into an abandoned house, and then recall the time when transplanted here as a boy for a week from the small town that had a vicarage similar to the one standing until recently (maybe still) below Černín Palace he had enjoyed playing tag amid the recesses of the Loreta's exquisite courtyard on Maundy Thursday of all days.

At this point I will allow him to lean for a moment against a wall bearing the sign *Waterworks Station*, so that under the starry sky he can drain a pint of Pilsner in the little beer garden adjacent to the Loreta Church.

If a poet, he shouldn't let onerous or attenuated ambition affect him, and he should refrain from writing! This spellbound man should refrain from writing, if he doesn't want what he has just snared to evaporate through all his pores. Refrain from writing! Unless to his mother, who has gone out to the cottage's yard disturbed by the cackling of geese, a letter comprising a single sentence. Better still, write this sentence on a postcard that would have been expressly instructed to depict areas other than the environs of the Loreta (the best postcard would show old Na Františku, which no longer exists, or a postcard of Golden Lane, where instead of a ring a cigarette holder was found). Just refrain from writing!

Let him follow the relentless and frightful howling of a single dog to the poorest part of the Střešovice district, into that swamp to get a brief glimpse (the wind has just extinguished her lantern) of a beggar woman lying down to sleep.

If like me, he will wish to die, if like me, he'll be susceptible to that delirious cavalcade of things eternal, or he'll bay like that dog who went silent right at the moment the lantern went out, like it, he will bay at the barren fields of the city, beyond which flickers the candle of the Střešovice depot, at the vegetable gardens whose strange beehives (they are not beehives, but he won't know this) resemble the garb of Tyrolean hunters, at the woods under which is built, with not a single sign of life at this hour, a garden neighborhood with vestibules in which white butterflies and shirt shadows frolic.

My advice is that he should let nothing discourage him, not even the fear that his drunkenness will suddenly be lacerated like that swampy darkness under the spark from the broken contact between the tram wheel, whose groove has slipped its line, and the electrical wire. My advice is that he climb up to the Church of St. Norbert, the highest point in Střešovice, to light the end of a cigarette that in the wind will go out in his mouth.

I won't chase him into the woods, that sparse growth on the Veleslavín hillside. He should just be aware of its swaying as he breathes in the peculiarly spicy scent its gusts bring to him.

Better if he veered toward the rocky slope where a laboriously constructed road collapsed five years ago and stare at the mica in the rocks covering this rotten carcass of surveyors' spawn. What might come to mind at this moment are the abandoned room with the bookcase and the story set in a neutral city whose name is only identified by initials. It will be easier to see those stones that have been lying here since the time when not a single house existed for miles around, only the few huts of watchmen who have been since recalled. He will see the stones more tangibly, and will remember that as a child rock quarries and herds of cows were what he loved most.

He will be tired. He will be tired when pondering the distance that separates him from his flat in the farthest reaches of Vinohrady. Let him surrender to drowsiness, to be wrested from it by two dubious pedestrians lingering somewhere close by opposite the windows of a house fortified by an iron fence — and, having only the distant lights in view, let him quickly descend toward Prašný most, the Powder Bridge, to imagine sitting in a third class compartment of the local train sleepily passing from nearby Dejvice Station. It would be better to let the tram sitting there an extra second longer, as if waiting for him to get on, drive off — and if he can, like a man gladly heightening his weariness of love, walk along the unlit fields to see up close a lighter area planted with heads of cabbage.

He will be tired. All the better. If he were not, he wouldn't have observed that the neon sign on a pharmacy announcing *night quiet hours* was flickering like the intertitles of the first film he saw at the beginning of this century in one rural tavern, where before his eyes a man who had traveled to the moon gets impaled on the tip of a spire.

I would advise against entering the wine bar emitting the muted strains of an old foxtrot. I would definitely advise against it. I would suggest instead to get into the nearest taxi he comes across at the cabstand, where it's been stuck for an hour, to be driven with eyes shut right up to the apartment whose aroma of kidneys was so imprudently abandoned. He will thank me. For no sooner have all the lights been turned on in the sitting room, no sooner have his eyes fallen on the page of the open book that had engrossed him before dinner, than he will settle with the full weight of his weariness in the armchair under the window, and his apartment will appear as a paradise beyond his wildest expectations.

I will not insist that he read. Yet he should hold the book in his hand. For what he will experience, casting his eyes into all the illuminated corners of his home, shall be worthy of the pages of this thick book borrowed from the public library. I would wager that he'll sit there through several chimes of the clock and experience some of the most magical moments of his life. Let him throw back his head and leave it lying on the chair's headrest for a while. Suddenly he feels happy at home and wishes the moment would last forever. He will desire nothing more from that day.

But for God's sake, he should not delay getting into bed. It's important to lie down when the night is still full. I cannot emphasize this enough! And leave all the lights on a little longer after getting into bed.

Sometimes he needs to stare at the ceiling to relish how white it is. If nothing else, just let it be white. Let not a single smudge tempt him, staring at it wide-eyed, into solving some rebus. Save it for another day would be my prescient advice. Nothing doing! He could also let his eyes wander over the furniture and toward the window left ajar, through which streams the fresh Vinohrady air. He should just lie there without indulging any thoughts! He will not indulge any. I can vouch for it. And I hope he left the book he'd started to read next to the chair from which his eyes had roved. Let him enjoy a moment longer the dazzling light calmly cast on the ceiling, then get up and extinguish it. He will quickly drift off to sleep almost as soon as he returns to bed. It will be a deep sleep. And the night will pass without dreams.

A car stops at the customs house behind Břevnov, light leaping over it (like boiling water over a cast iron pot, or like when buckshot hits a large bird circling over a hazy treetop), and starts again, with the speed of a bowling ball thrown down a lane of streaming rainwater, toward the city where there is a room with drawn curtains the key to which is held by the passenger seated next to the driver whose way is cleared by two headlights that shine into the eyes of a cat that has run from the horse butcher's door as evening descends.

To the right shimmers the greenish façade of a building in front of whose door stands a Baroque statue, stuffed owl, and Empire fauteuil belonging to the stock of a Břevnov antique dealer. To the left the sun slides groundward behind the Břevnov Monastery like someone doubled over in laughter. Then having taken a turn under the towers of Strahov (still a bit off in the distance), at the location of a people's café whose interior simply cannot be imagined, the car stops in front of the Pohořelec barracks where the wind is now fanning the lights of the gas burners.

Holding the key to the apartment he's been away from for

two months, the passenger jumps out of the car, which is not his, and looks around Pohořelec like someone with time to kill, or who is hungry, or procrastinating, or would like to line the wall of theater posters with paper, or wants to shoot a bird from the roof, or stand before the pharmacy with a toothache, if not like someone savoring the moment of his arrival.

Have no fear, he will not go to the convenience store and expertly check (like someone who wishes to knock over all nine skittle pins) a lemon's softness, nor will he give the butcher the one and a half crowns for the still warm meatloaf displayed in his window, nor enter the pharmacy to buy a bottle of Hoffmann's drops (isn't he writhing like someone with stomach cramps?), nor leave the drugstore on the corner of Pohořelec and Úvoz (whose window just lit up) with a toothbrush, for if he could take anything in that neighborhood it would be the multi-branched lamppost of gaslights.

If it is half past six and getting dark, clearly one of the two seasons not distinguished by either the extreme length or shortness of the day, if defying our trust in its reliability the clock on the Pohořelec barracks is running fast or slow, we will hardly notice since on the other side of the Úvoz wall the park extending all the way under Petřín Hill, where a small fire flickers, is tranquil, as is usual at summer's end.

The weekday meanders through the maze of buildings massed in neat array on the right bank of the Vltava like an insect on a frescoed wall that wishes to dupe the finger pursuing it, and the human torsos protruding above the upper third of the Úvoz wall are measured against the monumental buildings whose contours blur, against the spires of Vyšehrad, the bent nape of the National Theater, and the jutting Vinohrady Water Tower, if a flâneur is descending from Pohořelec toward Lobkovická Street, or Nerudova Street, down which horses hitched to a moving van stumble.

Here is the house with the Sun sign and the house with the Moon sign as well as the houses known as the Golden Star, the Three Fiddles, the Golden Key, and where the steep blackened wall of the Technical Museum rises up as beautiful as a pot overflowing with plum jam, the postcards displayed in the stationer's window signed by the soul of someone with death already behind him.

Why read for the third time in a row the inscription above the single-story inn, behind whose window glistens golden-brown pork roast and potato salad, announcing the availability of cheap rooms while his pocket is swollen (not a pistol) with the keys to a modern apartment to which he should now be going to finish smoking the stale cigarette left in the bathroom two months ago (an exact memory!).

He will not climb the stairs to Jan Neruda's small room, because he is no sightseer. He will not walk down a little further to the top half of Malostranské Square to enter the Church of St. Nicholas out of which an old lady is hobbling. He will not stop by the restaurant U Mecenáše, because he's in no mood to let the green eyes of an owl wink at him and to part with what little money he has. Besides, it's not the usual for a waitress to serve Beef Stroganoff and chilled wine to a Wraith. Nor will he go to the U Glaubiců tavern to slake his thirst for beer.

He will quickly cross Charles Bridge like one of its statues (whoever has not witnessed these statues quit their suicidal pedestals during the hours of night of certain days not marked in advance on the calendar to mingle among the nocturnal pedestrians, to get a glimpse of Prague's twelve bridges [all not visible from here] will never understand my poetry), his steps bringing him to where the bridge spills into the Klementinum, the three cockroaches, and while leaving it glance back at the Old Town Bridge Tower (whose archway cannot be passed under without a tinge of delight, especially if walking in the opposite direction, toward Malá Strana), before turning toward the Parliament building to ponder for a moment by this sarcophagus if he should continue to Klárov (what would he be seeking there?) or down Kaprova Street to Old Town Square, where he would surely open, as if a box of preserves, his eyes, bleached by the summer sun, craving past centuries.

Something memorable will happen as soon as he enters the square : either a student who has just started his fourth year at engineering school and is overcome by an inexplicable nostalgia will streak through Tynská Lane, where he lives, chased by one, then two, and ultimately eleven policemen, if not a lone ambulance that by some miracle has left its rescue station, or a widow in mourning will be carrying a large mirror under her left arm and a kerosene lamp in her right hand, the kind no longer in use, or crossing Old Town Square just then will be a man stricken by delirium tremens, a hoary pied piper with a horde of mice, if not a firetruck driving out of Pařížská Avenue on whose wheels the toothy cobbles will continue to chatter for some time!

What does this man want on Ovocný trh by the entrance to three nocturnal rooms (the leas reflected in his eyes will fall to the bumpy terrain of Ovocný trh and the cows will low toward the back door of the Estates Theater, in front of which stand three actors in makeup, and nude Guadeloupe women from the bar U Černošek will be fending them off with their polished-red nails, on fingers and toes), what would an enthusiast of the opera *La bohème* want here (one of its characters is just now entering the stage garret to sing the magic of the rooftops), which he steers clear of like he does any acquaintances he might run into on Na Příkopě Street (browsing the Panama hats, or waiting for the bus that stops at the Koruna building, if not going into the cafeteria for a snack of cold pork knuckle and potato salad), with whom he has kept contact to a bare minimum, such that he follows at their heels into a nearby cinema, where only a single movie is shown over and over and where he will secretly relish the sight of their faces (like someone running in dread from a kiss) while simultaneously looking at the same Wenceslas Square under which he's seated, though this time projected onto the screen, so that after his momentary respite from walking he could stroll along the terrace in front of Café U husy and see himself at five tables writing five different books and have a cab take him up Wenceslas Square past the Museum, on whose corner is a sere lilac bush, toward Král Jiří Square all the way to Grégrova Street, wishing to set his eyes on the window behind which stands his writing desk under a thick layer of dust.

He will not go to wipe off the dust. He will not go to open that window and air out the apartment. He will not slip his tired feet into house slippers, and he will not take a shower. He will take a walk to Žižkov to visit the exquisitely beautiful and long defunct Old Jewish Cemetery and there sit on a bench until the caretaker's bell signals closing time.

Was the clock at Pohořelec wrong? Were the gas lamps wrong? Didn't the afternoon matinee only just end at the edge of the meadow with grazing cows and Black ladies from Martinique (who I first thought were from Guadeloupe)? Is it not Wednesday? Is it not already late autumn, that the cemetery is still open and no one is throwing him out? Were they actually Panama hats, or just the white souls of multicolored felt hats (God forbid that stiff black hats should be displayed on white satin scarves)? Did the statues on Charles Bridges really change places? Is the sun not setting now (how would the high wall of the Jewish Cemetery and the lugubriously towering Žižkov tenements know what the sun is doing) — did the driver actually use headlights? Yet he suspects that at this moment the sun is setting, that if he were standing, at this moment, by the railing near Slavonic Island he would see it setting, he suspects, since the students in the cemetery (no one's been buried here for years) are now angling their books, since the water pump is creaking, since the bell has just rung to signal that the cemetery gates are about to be locked.

Once more he turns to the low little monuments — and like someone who has spent a lovely afternoon in the park and now it's time to return home, he gets into the car (his door is opened by the same man who stopped at Pohořelec and isn't a cabbie), which with the speed of a thought about obligations or ripening mushrooms carries him through streets he barely recognizes across Prague's food border.

He will not go home to sleep. He will not meet with friends. He will not buy a Panama hat. He will not have dinner at the butcher's on Pohořelec. He will do nothing that would justify someone to act in the same way as him. He will not set his watch by the clock at the intersection before Prague's Municipal House. He will not greet the man whose letter he owes a reply. He will leave for that open meadow now spread over Ovocný trh behind the Estates Theater. He will not go home to sleep!

From Bohnice, its tower a finger threatening the brains of recluses who desolately fasten and unfasten buttons on their way past the remains of Prague's ramparts (these buttons hang in accordance with the rules of mourning that govern the tilt of the head of those who think with the tip of the nose pulled downward by Earth's gravity), from that corner of it that appears to me as a grandiose casino and is inhabited by the most peculiar creatures, interned in a psychiatric hospital for certain stunning acts of the kind I experience in dreams and which, having intruded into real life, are rightly recognized as impracticable, at the very moment the inmates of this ship marooned above Prague are commanded to adopt the demeanor of people being served dinner, a crab crawls under the bars of the asylum's iron fence and, like someone backing away in fear of being attacked from behind, begins to trundle toward Čimický Grove.

This crab has precise knowledge of how the murder uncovered here several years ago was committed (let's not forget that its movements take a long time, like the march of imminent disaster, like a cure for anemia), which is, as far as I know (I'm no regular reader of the tabloids) still unsolved — it knows exactly what happened. It knows. It saw. Yet no means exist to compel this accidental witness to tell us, because the crab, into whose claw a pencil was pressed, has yet to write anything. (Such a method [if we were to let the crab crawl across white vellum] might yield a microscopic drawing that at first glance would seem to be a straight line connecting two closest points, if the crab didn't have to avoid, for example, a pair of cyclists riding toward the Kobylisy suburbs or the carcass of a rat reeking noxiously from that dismal grove — yet I have no illusions about persuading the crustacean through this or some other method to change its mind and divulge what it knows.)

It is certain that the young man who noticed the crab (probably the only other person beside me who did) took it for a reddened, prematurely fallen maple leaf. What sort of powers of observation should we expect from those who rush with lunch bag to the factories of Libeň! Let's not pester him. He wasn't off to catch crabs anyway. Nor to stick a drying maple leaf in his hat.

I ask nothing more from those stopping at the gas pump at the highest point on the edge of Prague to fill up on the way to Mělník than that they exhibit the most elementary decency to pedestrians walking past, like country folk do, alongside the ditches, particularly if a Sunday and the profligate gas station owners are in a hurry to knock back three bottles of chilled Mělník wine above the confluence of the Vltava and the Elbe.

Here's a driver, readying his vehicle early morning at the last station in Kobylisy, who would love to bring some joy to his child, so in his blue pocket hanky he wraps the crab that is struggling in the mud of the broken periphery roads down which we totter. Yet it might happen that while the man has to give his undivided attention to operating his machine, the crab, alert from hunger and its new surroundings, suddenly finds itself in the lap of a wet nurse or a priest (it would have pleased me most if the full extent of its body had covered a single page of the pastor's small pocket breviary). Such pranks are severely punished — and the crab would profit from it.

If it were not bound by moving unidirectionally backward, it could've headed toward the Bulovka Hospital for infectious diseases. But this would have caused a panic among the sick and the mass comings and goings of hearses from the hospital would have been blamed on it (if not on us). We shall not allow ourselves to tremble, even in desperation, for the life of our dearest creature.

If the schools wouldn't stuff all the youth into their bellies thrice yearly scrubbed with a rice root brush, the children of Kobylisy would have one more reason to celebrate for an entire morning. They would catch the crab in a hat. And some guttersnipe would kill it with a rock. I know what I'm talking about.

Out of discretion, so as not to frighten the puerperal woman on the way to the registration office at Libeň Chateau to obtain some document (I believe she would've been happy with a marriage certificate), the crab is carried in the mouth of the dumbest guard dog ever who will be very lucky its tongue does not turn into a bloody flame of ghastly ululation (maybe this genius thought it was a piece of desiccated tree bark it was in the habit of bringing as a message to anyone who thought to wound its pride) and who will do the crab, which has no reason to pinch, the good service of saving it from having to traverse the most squalid, rocky part of Libeň by setting it down in a particularly pleasant part of this working-class borough where no one ever thinks to stare at the ground and where the crab will be able to wait out the rainy season that immediately precedes Easter with its parade of pussy willows.

I've never heard of a crab ever getting bored. I prefer not to anthropomorphize. And I love Libeň (as I've said elsewhere) and refuse to believe that careworn workers would harass an innocent creature. It is more likely to be netted by a greedy local dry-goods merchant and forced into labor as scissors for cutting fabric (this ill fate, which I would wish on no one, was avoided). Besides, I don't know what sort of customer could bear to look at such a monstrous form of service, and none of those small suburban shopkeepers would have the means to properly promote such novel scissors anyway.

As for me, I wouldn't hesitate to head for Libeň to revel in such a spectacle and the artificial cherries of the rather tawdry hats worn by adolescent girls (I have never seen a more developed and at the same time tightly corseted maiden figure as I did in the vicinity of the notorious Strasburk Tavern).

The crab has no reason to fear. Nothing will happen to it. It can calmly browse the small stationer's with the round wells of watercolors stuck in tin casings, or arranged so that their labels can be read, if your nose is pressed to the glass of the shopwindow, Prussian blue, for example, or gamboge, which only pops into the mind of a mortal on rare occasion, unless someone on the cusp of puberty or a puerile dreamer. But since the crab does not know how to write, let's not entertain the hope it knows how to read. If only it could manage to climb the walls! It would be a silent witness to how unpoetic poverty is, even though the stories of the Libeň milliner girls are incomparably more engrossing (even more than the unparalleled allurement of pulp novels) than the fates of those relatively affluent daughters from apartments where privation is a stranger.

After all, no matter what we might tell ourselves (and this also applies to novelists who employ a generic template to write about the lives of the poor) we know very little about our fellow citizens who live in this district, which could be sketched as if by a compass that is the ČKD factory's tallest smokestack, if it were tilted and rotated like the tail of a cat, who has judiciously signaled to the crab, moving off into the distance toward Karlín, that it is of little interest.

A shame I wasn't walking right then toward Invalidovna to wait for my girlfriend, otherwise the crab would've been mine. I would've surely brought it to the café, just like I once brought a china doll, to demonstrate the cowardice of some of my ephemeral friends who like to boast about needling the bourgeoisie. And would it be such a horrible thing to place the crab on the low-cut back of some of those odious prisses who frequent the kennels called tea at five? Such a crab pushed onto the nose of a mendacious priest in a confessional might cause some pleasant chaos! I could also have its pincers pinch the neck of the hypocritical boss of the Spider, who one All Souls' Day afternoon publicly displayed in his scummy dive his sensitive nature in a way that would have merited at the very least some small form of public disciplinary action. I could've tossed it into the bed of my landlady, who brewed for me undrinkable coffee. I could've placed it in one of those pawnshops where I had to borrow a few crowns during the worst periods of my life. I could've created turmoil at the university. I could've placed it where it could watch over me as I drunkenly lurched from one street clock to the next off of bad sweet Graves wine. I could've instructed it not to let the bedbugs disturb my sleep in my rank lodgings. I could've used it as a device in a professional palmistry practice, which would've earned me more than one dinner at a time when I didn't have enough for food. With it in my pocket, I could've castrated my most marvelous appetites, the gratification of which has cost me more than one sleepless night. I could've sent it in a letter to the most idiotic critic. I could've taken it out to the country one day and sunk it into the holey riverbank near the mill under which is one of my favorite spots to take a dip, and thus give it more favorable living conditions than those where it would be confronted by notaries leaving their offices on the dot at noon, mailmen carrying humiliating payment demands from tailors, public servants who would much rather spit on this world, the bells of the Karlín church chiming for a wedding that will have the most dreadful consequences since it will be followed by the complete dissolution of the union from mutual infidelity, and where it would have to face the viaduct where one night I kissed a friend's lover with such passion that her body jiggled like an onion and awoke a werewolf behind a nearby chimney, who started to howl so menacingly we had to quickly shake hands and never meet again.

This implacable crab trundles past the Prague City Museum down Na Poříčí all the way to the threshold of the now demolished cabaret U Rozvařilů. I don't know, maybe it was the Hotel Bavaria, fixed in my mind as where Apollinaire stayed at the beginning of the century, and since this hotel slated for demolition has always struck me as one of the most poetic buildings of this quarter, I make a point of visiting it once a year, as if having arranged in a dream a rendezvous out front with my destiny in the form of a mysterious being, or as if an illustration that so moved me and has now slipped from memory, or as if an imaginary procuress who has decided to rid the world of me — I confuse these magical buildings in the same way I confuse playing cards and certain homonyms!

I know I could evoke that old Karlín tavern with a pianola past which I had to walk to reach my first Prague apartment, or at least the Karlín pocket park where a military band played every Saturday afternoon in 1920 like in Rimbaud's poem, or at least the night view of the Karlín church around which I wandered one time past midnight after the barrel of a gun pointed at my head had chased me from the home of a rather jealous man, or the hour when cars stop in front of the Karlín Variety Theater (whose interior reminds me of rolled-up sleeves tied by rose-shaped ribbons) and a crowd forms in the white glare of the large floodlights, not even half of whom have purchased tickets in advance, yet I wouldn't want to impute any of this to the crab, as if it knew my experiences, such as going down the stairs to a nearby urinal, or the collision of two heavy horse-drawn wagons at the Florenc intersection, no, I wouldn't want to impute any of this to the crab.

I think because traffic was closed off at the spot where the trams turn toward Masaryk Station the crab was forced (its movements are so time consuming) to leave its decorative lines and to turn at the Imperial Hotel in the direction of Svatopetrské Square, which for me is a stage created for dark midnight street dramas in which a bier has a role and where I would have liked to see for myself that peripatetic crab, which to the great benefit of my poetry might have begun to multiply like mice on that terrain of such anguish and perverted pleasure before the eyes of a man beset by delirium tremens, if it had not, or so I heard, crept into a ground-floor flat, where against my will I had to take a look, as I'm strictly governed by the rapidly approaching end of this pilgrimage that I undertake not without joy and with a crab-like patience.

I mentioned it was a ground-floor flat. I was mistaken. It was a bawdyhouse, if such an outmoded term, a bubbling mush of boiling black mullein, could be used for a room rented by three hookers as somewhere to bring their johns who were passing through the neighborhood, and apart from whom an old woman came by two or three times a day, a retired veteran of the prewar brothels who showed up in the absence of her three tenants (who wandered like shades, inanely asking for a cigarette to stop those in whose morals their discerning eye, impaired by an indeterminate illness, has sussed out an unhealed lesion to the surprise of an almost confidently responsive concupiscence), mainly to boil a pot of water in rotation to maintain a modicum of hygiene probably to comply with the law on preventing the spread of infectious diseases.

It is not known if this old woman went to buy coarse chlorine soap, or if she went to aimlessly kill time somewhere, but the door to this dump was definitely open regardless, and sidling in the crab, to whom we must shortly say goodbye, crossed the spot that normally would be a doorsill but in this instance was nothing that could in anyway hinder its movement.

Who would imagine that such a hovel would have a rug! I'm mistaken. It was just two runners, removed from the floor and rolled up into two cylinders. It's only because of this circumstance that what happened next happened. The crab sidled in, like someone tripping on a stair but stepping over it at the last moment. Yet right away it slipped, as if losing its footing, and fell into the pot of boiling water. Ah, if only the water were boiling! Set on the floor, its temperature had cooled to a degree that was not hot enough to kill the crab at once, but not to spare it either. At nearly seventy degrees Celsius, it was akin to a form of medieval torture.

I don't know why at the moment the pilgrimage of this fugitive from the madhouse was reaching its end all three tenants of the ground-floor room for debased men flocked together, and why at that moment even I entered, having mistaken it for a watchmaker's workshop (one building down). The crab was now dead. Two of the girls had fainted. The third looked into my eyes with such terror that I was walking around for a week as if under a spell.

I often return to these places. I enjoy the view of the sparse Čimický Grove from the Bohnice road. I like Prussian blue and gamboge in the shape of a wheel. I like the faux cherries on the hats behind the display windows in Libeň. I like the desolate space of Florenc. I like the Karlín viaduct. I like the view of that inscrutable Hotel Bavaria. I like Svatopetrské

Square that shudders in horror. I like returning to these places.

I will no longer make two-hour treks from the world's ten directions just to appreciate the length of Prague streets and match them to the length of my complex sentences, in whose meanders I have tried to develop several housing blocks to which I gladly return and which I've isolated from each other like nocturnal isles behind an impenetrable wall of syntax. This suggestive method (which I shall put to good use at another time when working on a story, or just a single setting, such as the Ungelt courtyard, which would suit more than one highly improbable tale, during the creating of which the storm clouds of my emotions gather in my head) seems to me somewhat tedious, especially with respect to the quickly disappearing stock of paper allotted for the expeditious completion of this book. Now as I am transported from one place to the next I will offer no rationale for the route taken to get to where I shall linger for no longer than a flash. Since I have thoroughly initiated the reader into my inner processes that have allowed me to master the exhilarating facets of Prague, I have every right to flit from place to place now. I see no need to pretend that I am serving up the story of a dragonfly who has strayed from the riverbed of my native village of sixty-nine houses to above Wenceslas Square, where the banners and those marching under them to the Sokol rally multiply with each passing day.

Last night as I was returning home on the No. 11 tram I heard a country girl quip to the conductor, who was asking passengers for their tickets, this good-hearted girl, unaware that her manners in this city were different from those of the ladies with blood-red lips clad in mourning dress, having no compunction to let everyone around her know that she didn't have a ticket and something else to boot : money (I didn't dare look at the face of my wayward dragonfly's country cousin, as I was embarrassed by the sneers of those who didn't understand her, just as she didn't understand them). Yet I, who lived so many years in the provinces, where the sun burns the skin differently than at the Klárov stop if we happen to be waiting a long time for the tram, might offer a brief thought on the situation. I know there are two separate, even contradictory sides. I understood the quip made by the dragonfly's girlfriend. And I also understood the sneers of the women with blood-red lips dressed in black.

This is why I can boldly say, as well as guess the reason, I have never had such a greater feeling of loneliness than on an All Souls' Day at the Olšany Cemeteries with the flickering of hundreds of thousands of little lights. It was like being in a city where I knew no one. Also fine. Yet my wistfulness was destined to dissipate at one of the lowest parts of the cemetery wall, looking out onto a November field, the visibility of which was reduced by fog. I will not go back there.

On one of my Sunday afternoon rambles, which took me from Král Jiří Square and across Žižkov, down Karlova Street all the way to the Powder Tower, then through Na Příkopě Street and Wenceslas Square and up Fochova Avenue, I had the opportunity to admire the garish charm endemic to the Žižkov shops selling cheap clothing. Walking in front of me was a girl from whose outfit I could see how someone might find this tawdry chic enticing, which would have surely delighted Picasso, and it brought back memories of Rue de la Gaîté in Paris. I wanted to introduce myself and imagined the kind of ideal Sunday magic that might come from spending two hours with her in a nearby hotel. I still reproach myself today that I didn't talk to her. In my desire for this girl I would at least buy a madras jacket from one of the Žižkov shops and be happy to save precious funds on a tailor. When my taste in this matter influences the young poets, several inner-city cafés will see a very pleasant revival of their monotonously sinuous surfaces, as I have suffered long enough from that dreary style concocted by expensive tailors of the likes favored by café habitués. I still reproach myself today for not speaking with that Žižkov girl.

I dread the vicinity around the Maršner chocolate factory. Never go there, unless some children's travel book has sprung to mind. Or if you're going down to Vršovice in the evening and walking along Ruska Avenue, which I can never neglect. I mean well for you.

I have long wracked my brains wondering why the side streets of Vinohrady give me a taste of ash and constrict my throat. I still have no idea why. There are no shopwindows on these side streets. Deplorable. If only it were a walk by long walls where you have a palpable fear that a dagger held by a perfidious hand will flash over your neck. I wouldn't want to fall in love with a woman from streets such as these. She would bore me. One day I would appear under her windows with busted head and broken cross. If I were Lord Mayor of Prague I would know what to do with these streets. Three times a year I would bedeck them with garlands and give free concessions to each and every poor person who agreed to run a stall for buttons, or floor polish, or haberdasheries. Or I would grant the Roma permission to overnight here. It would be a stark improvement. Make it happen!

I will consider lively Fochova Avenue with its vista of the Castle as the model for all the streets of Vinohrady for a long time to come. A swig of bright soda would refresh Czech poetry, rid it of its pathos. And engender a love of the universal. I think most of these blanched neighborhoods that sprang up at the beginning of this century should have rouge applied as if they were anemic lips.

I wish I could be the lunatic who kicked the majority of Prague pubs to the curb!

From the time a park was built on Purkyňovo Square that took up nearly the entire area, I haven't had the need to dream so often about Italian cities. O balconies, O nocturnal lakes, O smoked meats, tasting best when the evening shutters come down behind them!

After eleven at night when some of the streetlamps are extinguished, walking down Ve Smečkách Street gives me the illusion that I'm in prewar Prague. One time as I was going this way I got to thinking about putting together an offbeat edition of a newspaper where all the columns would be filled with reports from 1905. There is nothing wicked about a thirty-three year old crime. It turns into a dream, its reverberations no longer felt. And dated news about the steam-engine industry or post-symbolist poetry might not be all that irrelevant. The main thing is that not one of the readers of my poetic newspaper would have to fear war breaking out. Given humanity's frayed nerves, such a spa bath would do no harm if it were prepared by an expert hand. I am committed to it.

Whenever I see at night several of the illuminated windows of the Museum atop Wenceslas Square, I would like to enter under the illusion that I will encounter a sleepwalking woman wandering the centuries with a lantern in her hand. I wouldn't mind if she were one of those celebrated actresses from the mid-nineteenth century. A piece of black silk on her leg just so and a certain set of moral prejudices render love all the more voluptuous. In matters such as these I stand on immorality!

If I were to pass through all the cafés on Wenceslas Square while pretending to be looking for someone, I am certain I wouldn't find a single woman who was like me. Everything here is plagued by such a hackneyed form of prostitution. Unless a Saturday and I'm going into Café Pasáž on the second floor, frequented by the milliner and hairdresser apprentices, who still retain a sense of the romantic. After all, it is still the custom here to include dated operatic potpourris on the program, which like some older sentimental novels encourage emotional nostalgia, the most feeble trait of this century. I would kneel a long time before such a woman. In certain respects, I lack the courage to disappoint my fellow man. Otherwise the whole of Wenceslas Square, except its lights and lovely smell of must, can go to hell. I've had rotten luck here. Hear what I say!

I regret there are not at least a few boats below Podskalské Embankment that offer fried loach and Smíchov beer. I like frequenting this part of the city, but where exactly? A boat tavern with capacity for seven is where someone such as I would find the exquisite joys about which we don't even dream. I would go alone. Under the carbide lamp in such a wooden boat pub I would utilize my solitude to read the poetry of Tristan Corbière. I have no doubt I would meet several future writers there.

I will always have a soft spot for one forlorn wine bar opposite the exit from Smíchov Station. What I heard here from one of the most mysterious creatures I have ever come across! It made me grind my teeth. And I quickly drank the strong fortified wine. I should have downed hard liquor instead. Then the confessions I received here might have been even more harrowing and upsetting to my soul. Perhaps I would have run out into the smoky spaces around the station and laid my burning head on the cold tracks. The train arriving from Hlubočepy would never have reason to brake so suddenly. It would have been my final hour, do you hear, I admit it, and then on top of that the drizzle would make the wisps of smoke more blustery than on clear days. But since I was only drinking wine, the whole drama ended in a backstreet hotel. I was like a madman! I have no idea what would happen if I were to visit that wine bar again! Only now, when the paragraph has been written, do I realize that in a nearby half-empty movie house I once saw miraculously flickering trains barreling down the tracks in a film by Abel Glance called *La Roue*. Even today I visit that movie house. And you would be truly amazed at what seemingly insignificant impulses can bring on delirium. Be delirious with me! This is what I wish. Is there a greater sacrifice one can make for another than the most electrifying moments of your life? I don't think so. I don't think my lines will fade into oblivion without some creature paying for it with happiness.

If you happen one day to step inside that old cemetery in Košíře, don't forget while bedazzled by the birdsong to look over the wall into the first two windows of the building that houses a print shop. Maybe sitting there above a stack of paper and working his eight-hour shift will be one of those future poets. This is where I sat day after day for more than a year. I couldn't do it any longer. One day I got up and left, without even locking my office desk, to this cemetery and sat on a bench until evening. I couldn't go back. I went instead into the first barbershop I saw on Plzeňská Street to get a shave for the days when I would chase after the phantom of freedom. I still haven't caught it. Yet those nocturnal jaunts to Bertramka also have meaning in that they at least helped me become acquainted with the better features of Prague. And that is something! If this book is read for at least thirty years, then I would have influenced a good few thousand of Prague's more forward-thinking inhabitants. And even though I insistently resist thinking about it, the idea of writing my final testament, at least in some form, creeps into my mind more and more. Don't you protest, I am protesting against it on my own!

If you have just left a wine bar on National Avenue by the side of two seamstress sisters, one of whom exudes the seductive traits from the era of the cancan, and unexpectedly find yourself, as was the case with me one evening, in their apartment comprising a kitchen, where a calendar of Plzeň and a large padded ironing board draw your attention, and a room I would prefer to stay out of so as not to destroy my illusions, you will learn (their apartment was somewhere on the upper end of Fochova Avenue, so it was just a short walk to my place) what it means to have the 1930s transform into 1910 and Prague into Plzeň, or into whatever other nondescript city you have yet to visit and in which you wish to experience a trivial story. Such a dislocation will always be useful to you. You will experience an uncustomary dream, and you'll remember me. You will remember me as someone who gives good advice, at times in the tone of a whistling mouth and at other times in the tone of a French horn. I'm well aware when I should use which, and it has become part and parcel of my obsession that come what may I must fill Prague with all the chimerical beauties that cross my path during my short life. You will remember me, just as I keep you in my thoughts. But I wish you would forget, because only then, only then will everything that now floats in my spirit alone greet you all the more certainly within the walls where I sweat amid one of the sultriest June days of the year. One more brief sight — then I shall let you go. Because I'm in a hurry to stand under a shower (it hasn't rained for five days) and to go out to see for myself (when the mugginess abates with the final glow of day) the extent to which Prague, which I will be leaving in a few days, resembles my brainchild that has emerged from its invisible, or rather hidden, dimension. No more goodbyes to you. I did that last year. It's better this way. Otherwise I would never (believe me) tear myself away from these pages. And that's simply inconceivable.

On May 20, 1938, a Friday afternoon, I was sitting alone on a boat behind the restaurant at Mánes and anxiously scanning the sky as it became overcast and threatened to rain. I don't know what it was, but that day something strange was in the air! It was humid and cold. I hated having to throw my coat over my shoulders, I hated knowing a rainstorm was imminent, that I would have to seek refuge in the café. I am not a superstitious man. And still, on certain days when I'm unable to determine the exact cause of radiant or dark miasmas in the air I like to bury myself, in the same way we become immersed in nebulous doodles on marble tabletops, in the pages of an astrological calendar where all the planetary positions are given for each day. Please don't judge me too harshly for this pastime. Besides, a materialist approach, or so it seems to me, would detect with a precision we can only dream about today, once we have sufficiently sensitive instruments to measure the still unmeasurable, forces influencing the world and life that are much more bizarre than the relative position of the planets. On Friday, May 20, the firmament showed me nothing that could be called encouraging. The Sun at 28 degrees Taurus was in half quadrature with Saturn. Mars was in conjunction with Neptune in an inauspicious quadrature. The Moon was transiting the sixth degree of Libra and had its quadrature with Mercury and three sesquiquadrates with Mars, Venus, and Neptune. I had no illusions about what this day might bring.

The following day I learned from a variety of sources that a number of reservists had suddenly been called up to their regiments. Reports started to gradually creep into the newspapers about German troop movements toward the border of Czechoslovakia. Only several days later, when the immediate danger had passed, did we find out that our collective fate had been hanging by a thread. While I was radiating febrile visions of Prague and her thousandfold mysteries, which I will no doubt be deciphering my entire life (having fallen under her magic spell), those called to defend our country were already in position.

Today, June 29, as I bring this book to a close, a jubilant procession of teenage boys and girls was marching through Prague from five to nine, and even at this hour there is no end to the excited footsteps in the city center, which I really regretted having to leave. My window overlooking Král Jiří Square is open. I pause from writing every so often to look out of it. Although nothing could be seen in the heavens that would justify such excessive jubilation, although the Sun and Moon were transiting Cancer, although Jupiter and Saturn were inclining toward one another in a semi-quadrature, although Moon square Saturn was in conjunction with Mars (oh, were it not for its sextile with Uranus and Neptune I probably would have accomplished no writing today!), that distant rejoicing, now veiled in lights and drawing new resonances from the old sounding board of the city of astrologers, confirms to me more than ever that the days through which Prague is passing are days of her glory, days when she desires to be inscribed more illustriously than at any other time on the heart of the world.

What a magnificent feeling it is to inhabit this still, for poetry, virginal beauty, to which all eyes are turned today, which enters the eyes of writers from around the world when they gather here, eyes informed by a different kind of beauty — and for this very reason maybe more receptive?

I associated it with the emotion I felt when just today in the gardens of Prague Castle I heard several men, for whom beauty constitutes their innermost conscience, express their intoxication with the city. I made sure to ask one of them, whose approach to poetry is somewhat similar to mine, Tristan Tzara, if in St. Vitus Cathedral he saw the agates on the walls of the St. Wenceslas Chapel, two mentions of which in Apollinaire's work have guaranteed a second immortality, a new kind of immortality. In honor of this poet, I have borrowed the title from his story about Prague for this book. For me, his phantom sleeps in that black Hotel Bavaria at the hour when those who speak and write in his tongue disperse to their temporary lodgings. I am not able to express passionately enough how it was he, his eyes, veiled by chimeras, who taught me to see differently, to see everything about Prague anew, which not too long ago was the exclusive domain of old Prague romance novels. Fate has decreed that I come to realize this again on the final pages of this peripatetic book.

The ineffable magic of this city I walk through is beyond dispute, a peculiar mix of an acutely archaic charm and a modern sensibility. It is this mix that will keep Prague open in an especially intimate way to those who consider poetry the highest form of human delight, the highest because it has virtually no truck with the notion of practical necessity. How I detest the cannonry that might alter the ratio of elements that make Prague what it is. How every morning my body physically feels the pain of each blow that could be visited upon her. Of the blows that could damage the side of Charles Bridge, whose most intimate nakedness is presently revealed by floodlights. Of the blows that could rain down on the malachite dome of the Church of St. Nicholas in Malá Strana, which if illuminated, as it is today, by lights streaming from invisible sources seems to be my own head and the way it feels at those moments when it surrenders to the radiant emanations of inspiration. Of blows that might strike one of the masts of that dark, spectral ship that is Prague Castle. Of blows to the outstretched arms of Prague's bridges, beckoning us to seek protection under them. Of blows to the fantastic hats of the convocation of sorcerers that are Prague's spires in the dead of night. Of blows to the heart of Prague, her ancient blood staining Old Town Square. Of blows to many of those millions of eyes that are Prague's windows. Of blows to the lungs that are her parks. Of the least little blows that could rain down on her swarthy skin, the breasts of her balconies, the knees of her arcades. Of any blow that would make her take to her bed, inert for an indefinite number of days, an indefinite number of years.

Midnight has struck, and Prague lays her head, kissed by eternity, her memory stretching back to time immemorial, down to sleep, but lightly, because vigilance must be maintained on the watchtowers, at the lookouts, because vigilance must be maintained in sleep, so that not even the swishing of a bat's wings might escape our notice.

Sleep, Prague, and stay alert! Sleep and stay alert, just like a poet sleeps and stays alert. Sleep and simultaneously stay alert. Sleep, so that nothing submerged in the darkest cataclysms of deepest conscience remains untouched by the vortex in eternal motion like a *perpetuum mobile* machine. Stay alert, so that not a single glimmer of these mysteries is for naught. Sleep and stay alert, sleep and simultaneously stay alert, sleep and stay alert for the brevity of life, for the duration of eternity, sleep and stay alert.

PHOTO : V. NEZVAL

And a Prague flâneur (I, you, all of us), someone who is more than a permanent or temporary resident of Greater Prague . . . p. 152

While the language we speak, which we are fated to speak, might be incomprehensible to the world, which now has its eyes on us more than at any other time, the language spoken by Prague, her mysterious language, is comprehensible to all. My sole motive here has been to attempt a translation of this language into the words of my sensibilities, into the words my imagination has prepared for me. Perhaps I should have talked about what life is like in this city, discussed her mores, sketched the characters circulating through her. No! Do we not live in a world today that more than ever is subject to similar laws of social existence, if not the very same, almost the same? Are not the customs that we adopt and discard with the passing of time the kind that could be found anywhere? Do not those characters I've devoted so little attention to, if we look past their garb, harbor the same primal appetites as myself? It might seem that I have stripped Prague of her inhabitants. I only hope this is nothing more than an impression. Have I not bound them together even more tightly with the wax seal of my subjectivity?

One recent afternoon I had the alarming thought that Prague might have to be evacuated, and this had me imagining the city without people. Oh, try to envision yourself wandering around the silent streets with no living soul save the birds and insects! This bizarre dream was so vivid, a Prague in which not a single human heart beat. How loudly I heard the murmuring of the Vltava absent the clamor of human bustle. I realized, maybe for the first time in my life, that this snake was capable of emitting sound. I imagined Prague as an apartment of a thousand shapes whose occupants had left on summer vacation. Some cities do not lend themselves to such a fantasy. Without all their inhabitants nothing else is left. Not Prague. Prague holds up; such an image has little impact as she would continue to be a marvel even if spared over all our corpses. Because her destiny is to outlive us, to outlive us all, to outlive all our qualities through which we have never attained her grandeur, her mystery.

At another time, as I was crossing from Kaprova Street to that same little square (I don't know why I feel pulled here so often, to that very place where centuries earlier the people to whom Prague belongs seemed as if they would be subjugated forever), I imagined I was living in an age in which the astrological calendar nearly always indicated auspicious configurations, that the era of impending wars had already passed, that the era of hunger, unfreedom, the lawful destruction of one human being by another had already passed, that justice had already prevailed, that the seed sown in the blood of the East twenty years ago had already yielded its radiant fruits. I imagined myself sauntering through Prague in a time when human prehistory had arrived, in a time when the right to act and the right to dream were dispensed more fairly — and I relished the fact that Prague, imprecations flying over her flagstones, as they must, had remained true to herself, more than at any other time had remained true to herself! I saw her arcane beauty reincarnated in the people who will be born in a happier age for humanity than the era that has chosen us as the prime movers of time and revolutionary history. I thought of you who are still to come. I thought of you in Prague. I thought of you and your earnest or jubilant voices, which embody something of the voices of those marching youth who today have occupied all of Prague's sidewalks, crowding out all the traffic from her streets, rendering it utterly fatuous in these youthful faces, in the faces of those with aspirations higher than ours, that they will see how a justice much greater than we have known goes hand in hand with Prague's beauty.

Before I set down the pen, I would like to yield to the spark I felt blazing up in my spirit as I stood before that bridge in Leningrad spanning the Neva as an extension of the former Nevsky Prospekt, standing several steps away from the Winter Palace with a view of the Peter and Paul Fortress and the lighthouse, whose light mill would start up as soon as evening fell, when I suddenly had the sensation that my mind, so attentive to the delights of analogy, had migrated to that part of Prague near the Parliament at the end of Mánes Bridge with its vista of Hradčany, Letná Hill, and the broad swath of the Vltava hidden under her bridges.

At that moment, when the beauty of Leningrad and of Prague unexpectedly and solemnly clasped hands in my imagination, I fell in love with Prague in all her splendor, looking forward to the future. And in my mind then, my eyes fixed on dazzling white sailors kissing their girlfriends over the Neva as night fell, I gave an innocent kiss as well to You, whom I didn't yet know, I kissed You as my desire. Patience, please! Isn't the hope of such a kiss, now almost completely divorced from all practical necessity, enough for us to spurn all the justified hideousness of anxiety, each onset of irony and cynicism that tries to steal onto the edge of our lips? And if we are not destined to personally taste the beneficence of such a kiss, isn't the mere hope of it enough for us to experience everything that is happening around us today, everything weighing on us, everything we would like to banish from our lives, like the middle act of a drama that ends with the singing of an ode to joy? I have not forgotten the kiss of those sailors and Leningrad girls. I have not forgotten the light I saw blaze like a celebratory rocket over Prague when it appeared to me on that bridge in Leningrad. I have not forgotten it today, particularly today, when it's become imperative to draw on everything that could offer hope, when it's become imperative to array all glimmers of hope against any thought of hopelessness and despair arising from the awareness that tomorrow or the day after we might have to part with life. Yet over and above this very awareness, the awareness that we might be called to duty, called to enter her service, I realize, as her clock towers chime one-thirty, that Prague is eternal, realize how Prague is eternal.

And her eternalness, which I do not doubt even when confronted with a vision of her roofs engulfed in flame, bears traces of us, will bear traces of us. Do not be afraid to utter this last sentence, errant soul! Tomorrow a swallow will carry this sentence to the window you have thus far neglected to look at. This sentence will not be lost in either time or space, even though it will leave no vestige of itself. It will become something as moving and negligible as one of the small stones on Rabbi Loew's tomb. But it will not be lost. And if at one time birds wake up people and at another time people wake up birds, it's all good. It is also worth noting that black stones layered on top of one another centuries ago can sometimes stir the human heart. Who knows what would have befallen my brothers, those with whom I share a common language and a common fate, if it were not for Prague, if those who lived long before us had not succeeded in creating this talisman. This talisman, which has the power to mesmerize our eyes with dream, this talisman, for whose preservation we are willing and determined to take whatever action whenever necessary.

For the magic of beauty is that it arouses desire, and the magic of desire is that it wishes to be fulfilled. And a Prague flâneur (I, you, all of us), someone who is more than a permanent or temporary resident of Greater Prague, a Prague flâneur, for whom Prague has become in her magic something that has surpassed all practical necessity, all forms of self-interest, a Prague flâneur, under whose steps all the different centuries merge, a Prague flâneur, for whom it has become essential to think in chords whose elemental tone is the present moment and whose dominants and subdominants are dispersed in the vibrations of Prague's arcana, cannot abide the idea that he would still want to live, would still want to walk through this city, if the cobbles on which she is built were to be taken from under his feet.

But what would Prague be for us if our eyes were not gazing at her, at the color of her walls, if we were to let her sink, she eternal, into our oblivion, if we did not wish to leave our own mark on her dark beauty, the mark of our desire, now dimly stirring in us, if she were not to become in time, which flows, and space the Prague of our dreams.

I again hear the footsteps that in this book have preferred to resemble subterranean rivers than the echoes of female voices broadcasting on public squares of pianos, although there is not a single line over which their tenderness has not passed (at times as someone changing directions and at times as silence disturbed by the whistling wind of my unbridled memories). These steps know the virtue possessed by the person now rushing to address them again : at the moment he feverishly puts the French horn to his mouth, one of his frequent desperate moods compels him to break off and howl.

Oh Prague, I turn you in my fingers like an amethyst. But no. I just walk, and I see in the magical mirror of dusty crystal that is Prague the animated expression of someone who is fated to find himself and to wander, to find himself through wandering.

APPENDIX OF ALTERATIONS

By all accounts *A Prague Flâneur* was published fairly soon after Nezval delivered the finished manuscript, likely in September, 1938, if not early October. Italian translator, Bohemist, and scholar of Czech Surrealism, Guiseppe Dierna, discovered in the 1990s that actually two different versions of the first edition existed, and apparently what generally had been considered the first edition was in fact a self-censored, revised version, with the page count, placement of illustrations, and publication information on the colophon staying unaltered, as if only a single first edition had been printed. And the "ur-edition" was in such limited circulation that for all intents and purposes it was unknown and forgotten.

For the sake of simplicity, I'll refer to this dual first edition as versions 1a and 1b. The main distinction between the two is that 1b has the references to André Breton, Sigmund Freud, Marx, Lenin, Stalin, Surrealism, the proletariat and so on expunged, and in a few instances whole sections rewritten nearly from start to finish with multiple paragraphs excised. This occurs almost exclusively in the first half, and in two particular sections the cuts are substantial enough to necessitate the addition of extra text to fill out the pages to where the next section begins so that the book would not have to be entirely reset. For example, the longest section (pp. 71-87), the most pivotal of the book as well as its midpoint, was so bowdlerized by Nezval that he had to add three sections of poetry (two in verse, one in prose), thus turning the original single section into four. From here the two versions are identical until a few pages in the final section where his visions of Leningrad and Soviet sailors over the Neva are edited out.

We can only speculate what Nezval's (or his publisher's) motive might have been, but considering the Munich Agreement was signed on September 30, 1938, with the Sudetenland annexed by the German Reich in October, dispelling any illusions about Hitler's plans to occupy the rest of Czechoslovakia, it might be safe to assume that this would have played a role in the decision to revise the text to make it less overtly objectionable to Nazi prejudices.

While an argument can be made that version 1b maintains a more consistent lyrical tone with much of the political and ideological content removed, in particular the ponderous disquisition on automatic writing, we felt version 1a to be more historically interesting precisely for the expunged material. And in some respects the schism that occurred among the Czech Surrealists in March 1938, about which Nezval goes into tedious detail, is a precursor to Paul Eluard's split with the French Surrealist Group later that year over similar political differences.

What follows, then, is an inventory of the alterations in the form of cross-outs and revisions in brackets, where appropriate, and translations of the passages added to sections that were significantly expurgated, and thereby truncated by several pages. Some of the revisions seem to have been made solely for stylistic reasons, or to streamline a particularly turgid sentence. Most of these have been marked out, too. Compiling this appendix has left me wondering if sometime in the future a "clean" English edition of version 1b wouldn't be warranted. In any case, you can judge for yourself.

—J.S.

pp. 11-13

A long time has passed since I last sat — and alone at that — in this park, which will always signify spring for me, the springs of 1920 and 1921. In my mind's eye I saw Jiří Wolker as he appeared then, sitting on a bench in front of the Empire-style museum. ~~and before I sat down myself and pulled from my pocket the prospectus given to me at the publisher's just a short while before, the following inscription appeared on the bench before my astounded eyes:~~

~~Wolker and Nezval~~

During those years when ration tickets were still required to buy cigarettes, this was the park where new music enthralled me for the first time, where I would be reborn into a new sensibility. Evenings on Mělnická Street, giddy mornings and mad birds at dawn when returning from nocturnal trysts, Wolker's Café Finále, the charcuterie with its alluring student treats, the wickerwork bakery, and the crazy professor in the brown bowler — an incomplete, yet for me wildly exhilarating inventory of those years.

It's been a long time since I've sat in the park, and being here allowed me to return to my former sensibilities. I have always associated this park with a certain chateau garden where I once met ~~the poet Jakub Deml~~ [in my youth a poet], his house near to where my friends were living. This was later on, and it was a dismal time because you had to sit there in the morning or in the evening during the days leading up to summer vacation, like sitting in a park of freedom prior to graduation, for the women with braids to be different, so they would be new. I have never been inside the museum — what a quaint little chateau! Yes, you had to sit there like a student and jot down your thoughts in a notebook on bent knees, to compose a nocturne, an improvisation on piano, each moment presenting an opportunity to speak to the woman sitting on the neighboring bench — and then find yourself conversing with her.

pp. 13-15 : WHOLLY REVISED AFTER FIRST 3 PARAGRAPHS

You realize what it means to be a "flâneur" as soon as you're fated to be chairbound. The antithesis of a throne, this chair is a cobbler's stool, for working — and life is fleeting.

Maybe this is why the role of the "flâneur" seems so ideal, because life is indeed fleeting. When we walk — and especially when we walk with no destination in mind — the faint images of our desire impose themselves on our steps and prevents us from seeing its end, its converse.

The wait for something to ignite in me the expectation of a moment of joy, along with the rain keeping me inside, compels me to roam from book to book.

Some are so chained to thought that the object of contemplation is lost to their eyes in an excess of abstractions, which at one timed seemed unavoidable as soon as the discussion turned to poetry.

[ENTIRE PARAGRAPH EXPUNGED]

And I am saddened to think of all those ~~Marxist~~ aestheticians who, inundated by proofs ~~both dialectical and anti-dialectical~~, both pro and con, have entirely forgotten about the child in us~~, the child in socialism~~. [This child searches for a book in which he would find in the most intimate and audacious combinations all that has now and always been inscrutable to us, and only because it is raining, pouring down, because the intimate and miraculous things of our life have been surrendered to a squall, lamented by one of our pitiable rain showers.]

[FINAL 6 PARAGRAPHS ENTIRELY REPLACED]

[This is how someone discovers one legend or another, gloomy or touchingly silent, this is how a man chairbound goes out to wander in search of something he did not expect to see. I love the Prague of legends when I encounter them in this way. Modified as if for all time in old books with golden initials, these legends enter the streets and make me want to see them with my own eyes, as soon as it stops raining. What isn't magical about just sauntering into the Estates Theater without knowing in advance what is being performed right then to fix our eyes on the place where Mozart tapped on the music stand during the premiere of *Don Giovanni*? Or a day when the heavens promise neither a storm nor the blessings of cerulean leas to wander around the former area of Na Františku to bring to mind the charm of K.H. Mácha's sentimental journey to Márinka? On more than one end of a spring Sunday I went for a walk among the apartment houses that stand on the site of the former Kanálka Garden to look around if I might happen to see Mácha's old musician nearby, who would hand me a letter from someone dead. This is the sense in which I understand the term *tradition*, in which I see in a dream the mysterious resurrection of everything that is able to, that has the power to, no matter how forgotten, transport us in our purest moments, that is, when our desire returns us to the most distant memories of our nursemaids and the most ancient books, to the most distant memories of what we are ourselves, from a time simple song and the prehistory of old legends attracted our attention over the impenetrable confusions of daily life.

In this way our love of Jan Neruda might one day have us searching with the patience of someone driven by a hunch for that slippery spot where the great old man broke his leg. In this way we enter the little tavern where Jakub Arbes used to sit so we might see the color of the smoke and the window shutters on which his eyes were trained, behind which he gave birth to his "romanettos."

From the moment I read how Jaroslav Vrchlický would stand very early in the morning before the yet to open Ottovo Bookstore, this section of Karlova Square between Žitná and Ječná streets has held a new fascination for me.

Our century, those beautiful lights at night that ignite our lust, has enhanced the sensual beauty of Prague. Yet if it were not for the legends and the beings from past ages, to whom we are bound by love, it might seem that this new sensual beauty of Prague has somewhat deprived us of her, she eternal, different from all other cities of the world. No, as long as the fairy-tale power of love does not disappear from humankind there is no need to fear that anything of beauty will disappear from the world. Love is a magical power that resurrects what is dead, what seemed to be dead, what no longer even exists.]

pp. 17-18

~~When he graciously complimented my matching white coast and white hat,~~ [After we had greeted one another and started to walk, now together,] he began to relate an anecdote that ineluctably brought to my mind one of his illustrations for Apollinaire's *The Heresiarch & Co.*

•

It was this "new sensibility" that allowed me to experience ~~Moscow and Paris~~ [cities] in the way I did and not in any other way. And this "new sensibility" guides my steps through Prague today, even at this very moment.

•

The pilgrim and the flâneur, these two approximate expressions coined for one and the same activity, gave me above all a palpable sense of their distinction. It was not my lot to savor the joy of meditation. And the hunchbacked walker being ~~miraculously~~ [invisibly] conveyed from one place to the next was Josef Čapek's profound understanding for ~~my condition~~ [poetry buoyed by the marvelous].

pp. 20-21

And this is why I had long abhorred it! It was the cause of my misery as a student, which on top of the steady degradation of self-esteem and penury~~, almost always my own fault,~~ was perpetuated by the wretchedness of my rented lodgings.

•

The Vinohrady charcuteries where one and the same flavor topped all the others. And the alien streetwalkers, the alien university environment, [yes,] the terrible alienness that prevented ~~only myself~~ [me] from ~~hearing only~~ [perceiving] the ~~less vibrant~~ trumpeting of this quarter. The awful landlords, watching your every step, your loves, your comings and goings, your entire vapid life!

•

I could employ those old feelings of being unfree to conjure up images of heinous social bondage~~, for which the moneybags of this district are to blame.~~ I could put myself in the shoes of all the wretched victims ~~of this unjust social order~~ [of today] and thoroughly depress you. Yes, the ~~dispiriting,~~ anti-poetic side of proletarian and socially conscious poetry comes from the very fact that such poets have been so pleased to depress us. This I will not do. My philosophy~~, which is at one with the philosophy of the revolutionary working class,~~ is one of hope.

pp. 22-23

Evening is approaching. I am sitting on the back terrace of Mánes and the sun is setting behind Petřín Hill.

[ENTIRE PARAGRAPH EXPUNGED]

~~It was truly wonderful to sit there among people who had already made the revolutionary leap. The hope inspired, truly uplifting! Now, as~~ [T]he reddening sky between the hills of Petřín and Hradčany, the reddening sky on the Vltava to which I turn my eyes, brings to an end one magnificent summer day, [and] the sight of swallows circling the tower of the former mill fills me with anxiety.

And before I could register that I saw them as airplanes, one of them sliced across the Petřín tower and disappeared under the wireless telegraphy pylon only to remerge beyond the hill, flying off in the direction of Hřebenka.

If I had opened a newspaper, I would have seen so much ink devoted to the imminence of war. The threat of war, the threat to destroy all these café terraces, this Petřín Hill, these castle towers. The threat to destroy this city through which I walk. And maybe this is the very danger ~~that must be averted, no matter what the cost, and to do this the Soviet Union will sacrifice all its days and its good name; maybe this is the very danger~~ that for two years, two springs and two summers, has caused me to observe how a "new sensibility" toward Prague has been awakening inside me.

~~Having little to do with pathos,~~ [T]his "new sensibility" impels me to pause before Prague as if it were a violin, as if testing the tuning by quietly plucking at its strings, no matter what kind they might be. This "new sensibility" ~~lacking articulation and historical context,~~ has turned me into a tuner who converts everything he meets into a single tone, into the tone of an emotion without sentimentality~~, without pathos, without meditation~~.

This "new sensibility," which materializes in split-second encounters ~~no matter where, which~~ [with anything], ~~does~~ not distinguish[ing] beauty by ~~the categories of~~ important or unimportant, which wanders under the open sky and is at the center of life itself, this "new sensibility," without pretense, ~~without ethics, without aesthetics, and without utility,~~ has made me a Prague flâneur.

pp. 23-26

On June 21, the absence of one of those whom I visit now and again to request a [small] advance on a finished work that would enable me to live for a while carefree (not long of course!)~~, that is,~~ without a thought of what will happen tomorrow or the next day (this is how I live now, how I've been accustomed to living for years) presented me with two hours of nothing to do — and since it was one of those mild summer days for which I like to throw myself into the blaze of a responsive trance, my steps chose a circuitous route that I've taken with some regularity over the past three years, my delight still undiminished as if on this roundabout way I might meet with an unforeseen adventure, an unforeseen stroke of luck.

[NEXT 4 PARAGRAPHS UNALTERED]

You, reader, who might consider my reflections indecorous (yes, I too feel how little we have shared in the consumption of the wealthy's lovely tinsel — and I am well aware of how many have no prospect of a small advance to wrest them for several days from the grips of . . . but enough!), and so suspect me of social insensitivity, I can only affirm that ~~my European eyes witnessed in the most concrete, most intelligible way the nascent new Soviet optimism before the shopwindows on Moscow's Petrovka Street — and the appearance of this optimism in the eyes of Soviet men and women, in this concrete form, as they gazed at the miraculous multiplication of those dear objects, was not affected ("we produced it, we own it!"), but uncommonly ingenuous, even tender ("it's beautiful, I want it, but I'll get it tomorrow, or the day after, or when . . ."), uncommonly sybaritic.~~ [PARAGRAPHS COMBINED] ~~My antipathy to capitalists~~ [my revulsion of bloodsuckers] does not come from the belief that they have everything, that they have more than everything, that they have, could have, it all (with or without joy, but that's irrelevant), but from the belief that their "have" implies "not have" for the majority of humanity — and ~~the animus I feel~~ [my revulsion] will never devolve into the glamor they possess, whether great or small, and which we do not, cannot, possess.

As my eyes turn away from the empty, fraudulent, supercilious, or benign, though almost always heartless, ~~soulless~~ faces of the men and women who wear those beguiling meretricious trinkets, ~~for which I confess a weakness,~~ my absolute attention is directed at what shrouds the pedestrians on Na Příkopě Street.

[NEXT 4 PARAGRAPHS UNALTERED]

[FINAL PARAGRAPH EXPUNGED]

p. 28 : FINAL PARAGRAPH SHORTENED

These enigmatic lights were the first mesmerizing eyes that Prague cast on me. ~~And if apart from them I was drawn almost exclusively to other such lights (equally mysterious amid the darkness of obscure alleyways), lights such as that of the nightclub Le Chat noir, it was doubtless because behind these and behind them, invisible and yet present, present through her mesmerizing eyes, hid a singing Siren~~.

p. 46 : ONE PARAGRAPH EXPUNGED

~~And the awareness that in a land where the proletariat is victorious the student is no longer an evil who has to be subsidized, whose uselessness requires swift dispensation, but instead is a member of the self-assured army of workers, made me sigh and stirred my desire to make a promise from the future that the "bewitching" of the atmosphere I found in the Slovanka be destined for extinction and shift from the realm of life and reality solely into the realm of poetry.~~

pp. 48-52 : WHOLLY REVISED AFTER FIRST PARAGRAPH

I have nearly wholly abnegated any desire to decide where the wind shall direct my steps. My reward is to witness unexpected entries into places that with the passing of so much time have become very distant from the terrain on which my conscious possibilities move, granting me a dream, a peek at a film not pre-staged on any page I take in hand.

It was neither my choice nor need, paid for by self-denial, that opened the gates of the old St. Thomas Brewery, and on a Saturday no less, when its cellar tavern is at its liveliest. Someone walking through the quiet evening streets around Malostranské Square would hardly realize that close by is a place where, huddled cheek by jowl, young and old, men and women form a mob, which if pressed together like this on one of the neighboring squares would be the picture of a demonstration~~, and one hardly arousing any concern at that since why this faceless throng had gathered to demonstrate would not be difficult to fathom though unclear under what banner~~.

When I saw [one summer evening in the courtyard patio of a similar tavern located in the inner city] the eruptions of glee or rancor from this boisterous mass, ~~united at first sight by nothing more than pints of the dark beer that is a staple of this tavern, I couldn't help but recall a particular description of Adolf Hitler's first forays into political agitation, how he started in the cellar of a Munich beerhall similar to the cellar of the St. Thomas Brewery. Yes, it might have been among an amorphous crowd such as this that Hitler bagged his first modest game, the consequences of which have turned out to be so catastrophic~~ [all at once belting out a succession of ditties, my eyes were drawn to a group of about thirty young boys and girls who were clearly enjoying themselves here yet did not seem to feel quite at home. I could tell by the way they leaned over their long table and by their bashfulness, which had become somewhat emboldened, that it was a group of students who had traveled to Prague from some provincial town to spend a free day before the start of school vacation].

[FOLLOWING 4 PARAGRAPHS ENTIRELY REWRITTEN]

[Without any visible signal from any one of them, these thirty beings suddenly burst into singing, which at once attracted the attention of the whole tavern courtyard. They were singing a four-part chorale, a folk song, but different from the kind already acclimatized within these walls. It was exquisite. While a few customers were not moved by such beauty to break off from their raspy yodeling, their self-conceit, so jarring next to the pure vocals of these sublime young guests, was kept in check by the disinterest of those whose full attention was now commanded by the choir.

I was touched. How gratifying it was to see the pride of some of those, who loudly assume that as a regular they have the right to behave so hubristically, shrink before the pure tenderness of innocent beauty. And that chorus of young boys and girls, sublime! It was an innocence born in meadows. While I am not one of those folks who would appreciate Prague's pubs being turned into a barbershop quartet, still, on that evening I was moved. I felt that even where we might despair over the entrenchment of certain conventions not exactly of the uplifting kind, life continues to revitalize itself, whether we notice or not. Are not new birds born every year, do we not have the blossoming of youth around us, whether or not we're cognizant of it, always at the beginning, always reexamining everything that has already vanished from our aged eyes? Do they not come with hungry souls every day to the city, albeit more unseen, from all corners of our land to invoke the mysteries of Prague and to ever revitalize themselves with silent desire?

The young students finished their song. With sheepish modesty, they enlivened the place with two or three more tunes, and then, as if sensing that beauty shuns excess, they slipped away as quietly as could be from the tavern's summer courtyard and melted into the Prague night.

Now no one was left to impede the vocal exhibitionism of the regulars. And even though their old self-confidence was not wanting, for many of those who kept their silence the quiet echo of the country youth did not fade from their minds, feeling the same as I.

This is the impact exerted by each new generation of poets. And life wants it, and with it elderly Prague always resonates like an enchanted courtyard over which a lark is singing.]

When I observed [in this or that Prague pub similar to the St. Thomas] that [a] faceless, jabbering mass drinking dark ~~St. Thomas~~ beer, I couldn't help but see them as the source ~~even today~~ of that ~~outdated~~ mentality found in Ignát Herrmann's quaint little figures who ~~on such a menacing scale~~ still populate Czech films~~, as both the inspiration for and the consumer of these films, and how this particular mentality reinforces the burgeoning fascism. The excessive abstraction of thought in today's political journalism and the excess of abstraction in the schematic realism that has crept into contemporary social novels have veiled the true and active strata~~

~~of the reactionary processes engendering fascism, the reactionary processes that have so palpably found fertile ground in a place such as the St. Thomas brewpub~~.

~~It's unfortunate that~~ [I]n the hours when Malá Strana is still asleep a midnight miasma ~~proliferating in these~~ [that is kept in the] cellars drifts to all corners of the town, under roofs where it ~~will~~ become[s] invisible. To someone who encounters such a mob it might seem as if nothing's afoot. And if of a sentimental bent, then this or that old Prague song might spring to mind. Nothing more.

[FINAL 2 PARAGRAPHS EXPUNGED]

pp. 53-61 : WHOLLY REVISED WITH REPLACEMENT TEXT

There is not one person who hasn't experienced at least once in life that singular feeling of stupefaction upon returning home to an apartment where the furniture has been rearranged. For those who live in Prague, this city has provided many such similar sensations.

So one evening a year, National Avenue, as if rushing from morning to night in automobiles, trams, on bikes, rolling along to a point of convergence across Legion Bridge somewhere under Petřín Hill, is transformed into something delightfully inert, holding its left side still while the same undulating movement is performed on its right. Surprising at first, for some inexplicable reason, between Spálená Street and the National Theater, marking its presence with carbide burners enveloped in a lovely fog, we are presented with market stalls offering tawdry wares, which in this particular locale amid luxury shops has a theatrical charm. Even if you do not stop to buy something, the child in you will not fail to miss the imagery of a chromatic scale of pearl buttons, arranged in five, ten, twenty tones and going dim when passed by, like a distant cemetery on All Souls' Day.

At another time I had to halt my steps on the embankment opposite the side of the National Theater when I saw (it was right before noon) forest scenery rising up from the giant flat surface of a wagon and stick to that big bloated building, which for us springs to life only at night.

It may seem strange today in an age when the skies are filled with airplanes, but just a few years ago on the first day of spring I considered a single one in a sparkling blue sky, as it reeled in its line, the purest symbol of peace. This airplane was as poignant as the first violet on an emerald meadow.

If you ever wander to the Loreto at the moment its bells are clanging over the empty square, be sure you do not hear them while immersed in your evening newspaper. For the poetry of Prague, drowned out more and more by the platitudes showered on her, invites us to walk her streets as if we were walking through a deep forest or across a field the very last plowman has quit.

Not that long ago, when the most notable part of Prague was lit up with festive lights, I wandered across Kampa Island toward timber stacked on the Vltava bank, directly behind Charles Bridge, on whose stonework stage lighting was mounted. What I was looking at was the *fly system*, the backstage of a spectacular *féerie* of a Prague summer festival.

One night as I was walking with a French writer by the wondrous little houses situated between Legion Bridge and Kampa, this man, who knew the world, asked me who might be living in them. He was somewhat astonished when I told him the little homes over the river belonged to poor folk, because he had assumed, so he informed me, that they were the residences of eccentric millionaires.

I would love to experience once more the amazement that overcame me one day when returning from the zoo in Prague-Troja, having boarded the tram at the depot in Stromovka Park, I realized that, without our being aware of it, Prague is watched over by lions, tigers, leopards, and a vulture that bashes its head against a wire cage in the shape of the sky.

From the moment in the Karlín Variety Theater when I saw the Lilliputian men and women running between the tables and selling their self-portraits, I have been hounded whenever I pass this building by the image of the Grand Guignol, which engrosses my soul when I'm closest to my childhood, when, it seems, I am the happiest.

For us to know Prague's most hidden, enigmatic beauty, we would need to lean out of all her windows over her, and particularly those that are entirely lost in the most inaccessible places between chimneys. And moreover, this miracle shouldn't be approached as if we were tourists who have been told what to expect in advance.

I had the good fortune to see such a view from a ground-floor apartment located in the courtyard of a palace on Loretánská Street. The apartment had its only window facing the side of a building with five or six stories, and the most magnificent part of Prague that appeared to me in this forlorn window was literally blanketed with large artificial stars.

It's a shame not one of my friends lives in the corner house on Golden Lane, in the small room where we liked to drink grog while leaning over Deer Moat, above which old Prague was alight, crowned with a garland of pitch. How different the opera vignettes sounded here when played on an harmonium, how differently the clocks ticked here, how different it was to descend into a new city from this alchemist's garret. Prague poetry, now waiting to be born, its phantom tempting me more and more with every passing day, has in the city's most unexpected places such cages a poet could learn to sing in, to sing anew, to sing from the resonant depths of Prague, which convey to our ears the nighttime chiming of the clocks of Old Town, Malá Strana, and Hradčany, cages whose legend is no longer recited by even a single bird.

How wonderfully winsome and impracticable it is to swap every now and then contemporary literature, so tenaciously attached only to events we are witnesses to or victims of, for a volume such as *The Mysteries of Prague*. Such work, without even needing to give us the artistic gratification we rightly demand from books, offers more in some sense than does mere literature. They are imbued with the enchanted ambience of those places we are accustomed to walking almost impassively and hint at what's imperishable from the human imagination, whose superstitiousness, from a poetic perspective, is not its worst quality. Even though many pages of such books might be unreadable, their fustiness hides much real poetry, a real love of Prague, which wants to be revived and erected on a more alluring foundation. A wealth of intoxicants can be found in the dust of these pages, and when poets let the poison take effect, their work ceases to have that common generic character that encumbers even much good modern writing. What would Paris poetry be without that irritating dust it was swaddled in by old legendary

Montmartre! But Prague has *her* secrets. I am convinced that a day will come when her hidden, romantic, adumbral light will be the poet's keenest ally.

Awaken, you many obliterated Prague memories! If it be a dream, it is not only of today, which would so mercilessly subdue all our powers and all the prehistorical in us. It is solely to this prehistory that the present day is indebted if it is something more profound, more resonant than mere sensual pleasure or anxiety, if it is, or becomes, a poem. When the memory of Prague awakens in her children, in her children of today, her prodigious treasure trove of poetry will be brought into the light of day.

While the human heart flutters when the word Paris is uttered, why is your name, Prague, the most mysterious of all cities, usually spoken with derisive lips or vainglorious prattle! This is because each stone of Paris is marked by the kiss of romantic adventure under the sway of poets — and under each Prague roof they've been remorselessly disfigured by the feisty hydra of banality. And yet I have always felt that despite the deplorable twaddle of a Kondelík, you, city of a hundred spires, still halfway submerged in hoary legend and donning before our eyes a magical garment spun from the lights of this year's spring, are able to serve poetry, which we love, by investing it with both your old magic and your youthful irresolution. Such is how I learned to love you, to call your bridges and streets by their true names, so that I might awaken in them something akin to a spell. My subjective life, endlessly craving rapture, has tried to make you the stage of my desire and a vocabulary rich enough to express the color of our mad loves, our yearnings.

In this city, in the diagram of the shortest link between two points on the map of straight lines called real life, on the ground plan of this city that fate has awarded you, at unexpected moments you have encountered astonishing spectacles, creatures who suddenly seemed unearthly. These encounters have occurred when you have stepped onto the stage of improbable fairy plays, when you have experienced festival lights, had the illusion of something seen long ago, so that you stopped walking from point to point, from destination to destination, and saw the city called Prague in that spectral form it had when you were viewing it through a peephole.

If we are to live, if we want to, if we must live, how would you not try to rekindle the magic log of legend when you yourself have been ensorcelled by the shadow play of its flames. And if your life has been less desperate, much closer to vertigo and daydream than before from the moment you have been guided by the bewitching eyes of your Prague hallucinations, you would like to infect all Prague flâneurs with your hard-won bliss.

[2 ADDED SECTIONS TO FILL OUT THE PAGES]

Once again I stop before the entry to Prague Castle to take the opportunity to incline over the low wall above several crinkled roofs and surrender myself (how many times already?) to the panorama of Prague. It should come as no surprise that this is the very spot where my poetics most often learned to embrace this city with the long arms of verse. If you observe Prague from here, as her lamps light up one after another, you feel the urge to dive head first into the illusory lake where a magical castle of a hundred towers has appeared. I nearly always have this sensation whenever the vesper bell reaches me over this black lake of sidereal roofs that I once associated in my mind with the image of an absolute defenestration — and now allow me to recreate this vision on the pages of this book :

The vesper bell rocked the cannonade
and the sun
striking the St. Vitus windows
deluged Hradčany's cathedral
the altars hissing amid hell
and only in the St. Wenceslas Chapel
did the bluing tremolo of evening
purl

Buttressed by the last rays of the waning day
I noticed the onset of dusk
when the evening star
like an eternal light
supplanted the afterglow dissolving in the azure

I stood on the Old Castle Steps
and while medieval windows buckled like talismans
I saw in the mist a giant ship
that was Prague

Neon ads hopped along the towers
like fair-haired monkeys between masts

the cuneiform of perfumeries spilled into the night
a fountain spouted over the river
and trams extinguished their lights in transit circles

It was a city of frivolous cheer
on whose observatories
eternity
a pearl mussel
for centuries cavorted with necklace along the mirrors
always the same mysterious caryatid
invulnerable to the telescopes of royal magi
despite treacherous signals
that determined the fate of newborns
eternity
a bluebottle
at the queen bee's intemperate feast
who casts a swarm
it was a city of frivolous noise
igniting its nightly fireworks

It was a grim ship under attack by corsairs
from all corners of Europe shelling Hradčany's towers
that ancient and defiant mast

The music of a relay baton
that whores passed to pedestrians as ordered
contended with the vesper bells
that dispersed contagion
and a raft of gases creeping over the gutters

The patrolmen scattered and the castle guard fell asleep

I was amazed to suddenly see
in the windows of the old Chamber of Parliament
a shadow
that cast into Deer Moat
figures of masked chimeras

Oh ancient eons
the precipitous void of the mirrored labyrinth
the ghost that has kept me from sleep for all time
shambling through my life in terror
as if walking a tightrope
of death
oh deceptive mirage
I've been waiting for
and no longer seen by any of you
blessed dead gaunt as greyhounds
all of you old religions
bastards of the royal realm
of eternity
of death
I cast you out, cowled scarecrows
and swooping on them
a shadow
finished an ancient defenestration

p. 66

. . . — letters from my friend Jiří Mahen, which allowed me ~~to nourish~~ [not to lose] the illusion that I am a poet.

pp. 71-87 : WHOLLY REVISED

Before this book imbibes a few more drops of the sleeping potion of cinnabar surprises (although I'm especially fond of the indescribable brown of old window frames in the little houses under Charles Bridge near Dražický Square, where I was particularly taken with a small balcony for three suspended from a wine restaurant), and before I make another attempt to uncoil the snake of medieval turrets from around me, I would like to revise a number of principles I adopted as my own ~~on the first pages of *Invisible Moscow*~~ [some time ago] (as if my steps weren't nearly always driven by inner impulses that one way or another convincingly defined said principles), and, with eyes fixed on my present paths, confirm or refute a few fundamental ideas ~~for which Surrealism has had a thing or two to say~~ [that touch on them].

But first allow me to refererence ~~something Marx asserted, namely, his~~ [the] perfectly justifiable bias [held by noble spirits] against "practical necessity," which ~~he~~ [they] rightly ~~saw~~ [see] as synonymous with avarice, to underscore that only as a direct consequence of the universal blindness ~~engendered by capitalism~~, having fetishized "practical necessity," human life and the productivity of the human spirit are valuated, even by those souls who have their sights on a more just future, far too exclusively by the degree to which they serve such "practical necessity."

[ENTIRE PARAGRAPH EXPUNGED]

If intoxication is inarguably ~~an emotional~~ [a poetic] aspect of reality, which could be subsumed under the concept of dreaming, a most sublime beauty, one of the highest values of life, now understood outside the realm of practical necessity, that thousandfold avarice [in which] ~~coloring the bourgeois pursuit of~~ joy in life [is sought], if beauty derived from dreaming is a return to the most intrinsic ~~domain~~ [realm] of life, as it wishes to elevate itself to unprecedented heights ~~via socialism~~, then we cannot avoid the question if dream is, or could be, ~~as André Breton would have it,~~ the father of action, or if there exists ~~a terrain~~ between dream and action ~~whose excavation could be linked to the violent intervention of our will~~ [a wall that will be difficult to bring down].

When discussing the word "action" let's not ~~get side-tracked by classless society, the~~ [allow any] anticipation ~~of which only~~ [to] trigger our impatience, but look instead for the content of ~~"action"~~ [this word] in everything, the heroic and unheroic, that falls within the ~~purview~~ [domain] of external exigency, whereupon for dream and dreaming we reserve a domain of the highest inner "freedom," a "freedom" that manifests only in this domain~~, which will presumably remain reserved even in a world where the sphere of external exigency is dialectically transformed into the sphere of external freedom~~.

To keep from dwelling too long in abstraction, allow me to quote Plato ~~as paraphrased by Freud~~ that, "The virtuous man contents himself with dreaming that which the wicked man does in actual life."

[ENTIRE PARAGRAPH EXPUNGED]

If, for example, the performance of criminal activity in dream~~, originating in infantile desires,~~ is more marvelous in the poetic sense than all those ~~dark~~ [bleak] moments spanning the era of classical tragedies to the Gothic novel and roman noir, if this ~~bloodstained~~ aspect of dream, so close to the greatest poetic spirits such as ~~Sade~~ [Mácha] or Lautréamont, has ~~a virtuality~~ [an aesthetic expressiveness] whose power is beyond doubt, then what sort of approach should be adopted by those of us who ~~share with Marx the belief in the need~~ [would like] to change the world for the better, how should we approach these dark aspects of dream, when~~, as Breton assumes,~~ its tentacles genuinely incite action, [that is, a malicious dream a malicious action].

Let no one gainsay me that I'm conflating a normative ethical position with an empirical position, and that I wish to obfuscate empirical consequences by such a normative ethical perspective. I categorically refute this. I only wish to ~~vividly evoke~~ [offer a tiny example of] what must be confronted if we are to acknowledge the power of dream to influence action.

Fortunately, the dream has remained for poetry what it was for Plato, a boon whereby even the greatest evil can exert a ~~salutary~~ [non-evil] influence, ~~and what it was for Freud, wish fulfillment, or~~ a kind of action, in and of itself, a consummation of action~~, action innately capable of fulfilling our desires~~.

[ENTIRE PARAGRAPH EXPUNGED]

~~So with dream conceived in this way~~ [With this opposite conception of dream,] what's projected onto the screen of a future ~~classless~~ [more harmonious] society ~~in the minds of Surrealists~~ might be conditions that ~~such a classless~~ [no] society would ~~neither~~ be obligated ~~n~~or justified to satisfy. If ~~it is a fallacy to localize~~ the conditions for a "liberation of the mind," as ~~applied~~ [derived] from the "liberation of dream," [are localized] to a future ~~classless~~ [harmonious] society, then the ~~present~~ consequence of this error is [and will be] ~~the~~ [overwhelming] disillusionment ~~among Surrealists with the~~

~~evolution of Soviet reality, whose categorical fate is the fact that it is reality and has absolutely no reason to approximate the realm of dream~~ [as the evolution of human society remains and will remain forever in the realm of reality and does not have in its power the ability to relocate to the realm of dream]. ~~Freedom conceived under the sway of~~ [The concept of freedom as derived from] the "liberation of dream" cannot be of the kind that ~~in any way might be reconciled with~~ [could be realized in the realm of] social reality. Through the ability to sublimate, the people of ~~socialism~~ [a more highly organized society] have and will have no other choice but to again isolate their galvanizing ~~asocial~~ [primal] desires to the inspired s~~phere~~ [realm] of dream and the ~~sphere~~ [realm] of poetry, because the design of social reality has no place for the ~~dialectical~~ synthesis of reality and dream~~, for surreality~~.

For that matter, reality and dream cannot be considered ~~dialectical~~ [legitimate conceptual] antitheses. Whereas reality either exists or it doesn't, whereas there is only one reality, whereas reality is all that does exist, dream in and of itself cannot be placed on the same conceptual scale, on the same conceptual plane, as if it were reality's antithesis, because dream is itself a product of reality, a particular form of reality-processing in the human mind.

~~Given Freud's view of dream as disguised fulfillment of repressed wishes — and whereas~~ [While it is said that] the dream owes its magical structure to the censor of consciousness, which after all announces itself during waking precisely because it acts to repress these [primal] desires — the dream will remain [in human society] ~~wholly~~ confined to ~~its own realm~~ [sleep] and then to those rare moments of waking life in which, because right at that moment we've ceased to be ~~an agent~~ [a person] of action, we become a dreaming ~~subject~~ [individual], a poet.

The life-giving power of dreaming will be ~~granted~~ [welcomed more justly by] humanity to the extent it ~~is allowed to~~ becomes truly human, a humanity for whom the right to life will be more equitably distributed between the right to act and the right to dream. ~~No~~ [Every] human society (the more progressive the society, the ~~less~~ [more] likely the chance) will ~~concede that~~ [strictly differentiate] these two rights — the right to act justly, corresponding with social necessities, and the right to each dream, in which ~~the subject would fulfill~~, in the dream context, ~~repressed wishes — exist in a notional causal unity, as Breton's sees it~~ [primal desires are fulfilled].

~~Let us look then at all that is entailed in resolving the reality-dream conundrum as expounded by the founder of Surrealism.~~

In addition to muddying the idea of a ~~classless~~ [more highly organized] society by introducing a conception of freedom colored by dream, thus giving rise to disillusionment with the evolution of ~~socialism as is~~ [it] as dictated by its struggle with all manner of temporal exigencies, ~~Breton's conception of dream and action as communicating vessels~~ [the incorrect conception of the relationship between dream and action] informs ~~his attempt to to create a causal connection~~ [a tendency to see a straightforward connection between] social emancipation and the liberation of the mind, whereby the level of the liberation of the mind~~, for him,~~ is [here] measured by how it manifests in the dream realm. If ~~through and in socialism~~ [in a more highly organized society] the mind is emancipated [ever] more from [nefarious] economic ~~determinants~~ [dependencies]~~, from property relationships in the context of private ownership~~ and hucksters of all stripes, then ~~a socialist system, and not even one that has reached the stage of communism,~~ [it] does not and will not substantially alter humanity's ~~unconscious~~ [primal subjective] desires, for which the ~~sphere~~ [realm] of dream, the ~~sphere~~ [realm] of dreaming, will continue to be a space rigorously reserved, more rigorously even than ~~under the brutality of an unbridled~~ [in] laissez-faire ~~capitalist~~ system[s].

I consider it to be a sign of the general progress in social empathy and tastes the ~~fact~~ [circumstance] that from the era of Romanticism to our present day poets have so honed the censorship of consciousness in themselves that they scorn the dream fulfillment of their egoistical social desires, ~~from the approbation of petty bourgeois idyllicism to the bourgeois appropriation of their mistresses;~~ they have so honed the censorship of consciousness in themselves that in their disdain for ~~the idyllic~~ [petty socially egoistical] happiness ~~of petty bourgeois daydreamers~~ their deep, unconscious primal urges are fulfilled in their poetry through the method of disguise and ~~by utilizing~~ [with the help of] mechanisms analogous to ~~those of the dream-censor~~ [dream].

We now come to the question of so-called waking dreams, which ~~according to Breton's initial definition of Surrealism are "pure psychic automatism." Even though he revised his definition, albeit en passant, when he recommended in his Second Manifesto of Surrealism that Surrealist writers be mindful of the division between the conscious and the unconscious that arises during écriture automatique, from the~~

~~philosophical point of view Surrealism has yet to satisfactorily clarify and precisely establish to what extent the conscious process of writing might absorb into itself aspects of the unconscious~~ [are said to be the fruits of "pure psychic automatism," and it needs to be decided to what extent the conscious process of writing is influenced by it].

~~Here as well we might turn to Freud for guidance since it was he who discovered that unconscious wishes are able to penetrate the waking state, that our involuntary thoughts are responsible for virtually inducing a series of accidental associations, pointing to an imperative unconscious source, and a variety of faulty actions contend to fulfill our unconscious desires even during waking.~~

~~Despite Freud's irrefutable findings, this is~~ [We are certainly] still a long way from being able to speak of waking activities, which includes poetry, as *pure* psychic automatism. ~~With the classics, for which an a priori rational conception of the work was an absolute requirement, it is no coincidence that irrational images distorted by the censor keeping watch over the unconscious surface only rarely.~~

If we take the displays of mediums, for whom poor technical training presents no obstacle to creating either paintings or written work, relatively speaking, as products [of the spirit] of the most automatic kind, then we will surely notice the extent to which these products are ~~rationally~~ influenced by the naive dogmas of occultists and the extent to which they are linked, even in expression, to their own spiritualist tradition.

So when scrutinizing ~~the~~ automatic [literary] texts ~~of Surrealists,~~ the prevalence of a common quality is infallibly detected, and the rather monotonous similarities are not ~~first and foremost~~ the result of unconscious impulses penetrating the waking state, but instead are largely the product of an analogous verbal technique, an emphasis on a similar aesthetic effect, drawing on stylistic devices borrowed from the Rimbaud-Lautréamont poetic tradition, imbued with the spirit of Apollinaire and of Dada, ~~where~~ [in which] the programmatic incorporation of chance has facilitated the standardization of this given [characteristic] style through the random combination of verbal elements.

If ~~Surrealist automatic texts are compared with so-called Surrealist puns, or the game known as Exquisite Corpse, we find that the role played by chance is similar to poems created by pulling words out of a hat, which was the most authentic expression of Dadaism. Given these games have had an impact on the Surrealist idiom, and given their techniques were already employed by~~ Apollinaire in his poem ~~“The Windows,” whose individual lines are created by different writers, then psychic automatism cannot be given unequivocal priority in Surrealist prose or poetry since “objective chance” plays such a crucial role in their creation, and additionally,~~ [we] consider~~ing~~ how decisive for ~~their~~ [the] creation [of such texts] is the ~~Surrealist~~ [poet’s] proclivity for a particular mode of expression, ~~a Surrealist text or poem~~ [then these texts], these putative waking dreams, ~~are nothing at all like~~ [cannot be equated to] night dreams either in terms of inception or in terms of structure.

While much of what defines ~~a Surrealist text or poem~~ [them] is the outgrowth of a mannerism established with the help of partial psychic automatism, objective chance inherited from Dadaism, and ~~the dictates of style~~ [certain tastes], while ~~the Surrealist~~ [a new poetic] genre was formed on the basis of this complex of influences, ~~just as the fairy-tale genre, for example, is defined by an array of specific elements, then~~ [we cannot consider objectively binding (in the sense of a valid principle) a variety of directives and proscriptions, a variety of] ~~Surrealist~~ pieties — such as the prohibition on a preconceived motif, the prohibition on meter and rhyme, the prohibition on a conscious focus on this or that effect— ~~cannot be understood in the sense of those legitimate directives and proscriptions that come from within, that are derived from the inherent laws of the poetic process itself~~.

Given our knowledge ~~of Freud's dream discoveries,~~ that the most insignificant experience from the previous day could serve as a dream trigger, we might analogically assume that absolutely anything could serve as a poem's motif. The main question is how much [inner necessity and] dream capacity~~,~~ ~~derived from the power struggle between unconscious impulses and the censor keeping watch over the unconscious,~~ will this motif, corresponding to the previous day's experience, be subjected to through a processing [that would be] ~~analogous~~ [similar] to the operation of dreamwork.

If a real connection ~~is induced~~ [exists] between the poet's intellect and unconscious desires when creating a poem on the basis of a preconceived subject, and not, above all, on a preliminary aesthetic orientation toward a particular idiom, a particular type of image, a particular sequencing of verses, ~~in other words,~~ a ~~Surrealist~~ [particular] style, then this subject, however and for whatever reason it was conceived, even if rationally, and however and whatever its intended effect, will be transformed through the ~~dialectical~~ confrontation between conscious and unconscious psychic ~~tendencies~~ [forces] into a "waking dream" whose consequent form is neither a product of the subject, nor from its choice, nor from anything predetermined.

If the consequence of ~~Surrealist~~ [this or that poet's] mannerism and preferences is that meter and rhyme are excluded from poetry as a legitimate matter of style, then from the moment we realize that ~~Surrealist~~ [such] texts are not and cannot be [an expression of] pure psychic automatism, the principle that holds meter and rhyme to be artificial impediments to the supposed actual functioning of thought has no applicability, and if utilized or not, their usability or non-usability, is a matter [of the poet's] relative stylistic inclinations ~~of the poet~~.

[ENTIRE PARAGRAPH EXPUNGED]

Having ~~succeeded in shattering the notion that Surrealist activity is an expression of pure~~ [managed to create the proper context for the question of] psychic automatism, ~~having viewed~~ [such that we see] the work of poetry not as a passive reflection of the "actual functioning of thought" but as an artificial creation that in our century has extricated itself from the predominant influence of rationalism to find itself in ~~the domain of~~ [intimate contact with] the imagination [and its realm], which blossoms in the freest and most complete way in dream, and ~~having divested the poem of its~~ [no longer unilaterally overestimating the poem's] ostensible determinacy by *pure* automatism~~, overestimated by Surrealism, to treat it dialectically~~ [but seeing it instead] as an aggregate of the poet's conscious and unconscious propensities, we are then able to tackle anew the question of poetry as directed or undirected.

[2 ENTIRE PARAGRAPHS EXPUNGED]

~~It follows from what I have outlined above that~~ [T]he poem, a product of the poet's sensibility in its entirety, directed by a poet's intellectual and uninhibited obsessions, finding in the imagination and in the arcanum of dream its unforeseen marvelous, its ~~oneiric~~ [dreamlike] marvelous, ~~that~~ the poem, this child of intention and chance, of passion and a desire for rapture, consciousness, and sleep itself, is an expression, to the fullest extent possible, of the poet's spirit, what the poet wants and knows with what is innately desired and unsuspected.

[ENTIRE PARAGRAPH EXPUNGED]

A malign dream that is a social good because ~~the dream~~ [in it one] is gratified [solely] by the *dreaming* of evil, [the actual perpetrating of] ~~which~~ is rightly excluded from the ~~sphere of action~~ [realm of real life, poignantly] goes hand in hand with good ~~in the most poignant way we have ever known~~ in the work of Lautréamont — in *Les Chants de Maldoror* ~~dialectical~~ good in the thrall of a dream of evil and in *Poésies* the ~~codification~~ [enactment] of good in the conscious sense — and what this work ~~of works~~ accomplishes in both its monumental and seemingly incongruous parts is a ~~grand~~ [spectacular] integration of the poet's mental state. If in *Maldoror* one is denuded of unconscious desires, which are fulfilled through a sovereign catharsis that is an end in itself, in *Poésies* one is [deliberately] placed in opposition to emotional megalomania and ~~the~~ negativism ~~of Romantic conceptions of humankind~~ in the service of hope, in the service of good, to the limits of human necessity.

For that matter, ~~compared to all other poetry~~ [what makes] *Maldoror* [so great in other respects] is ~~unrivaled in~~ its fantastic balance between its intentional design, which is an attack on both the man and the creator in the name of good vs. evil [between the intentional design,] ~~as~~ directed by the poet's conscious obsessions, and its ~~oneiric aspect,~~ non-predetermined [dreamlike aspect], ~~and~~ gushing out during the very process of creation from under the pen of the person writing. Even though, "A man or a stone or a tree is about to begin the fourth canto" of *Maldoror*, it begins face to face with Isidore Ducasse, who never lets his mind wander even for a moment from what his song is and should be.

While the ~~incomparable~~ magnificence of *Maldoror* is ~~inherent in~~ [a result of] the utterly active approach taken by Lautréamont for its composition, ~~with~~ [and of] conscious forethought of its ultimate meaning and impact, the [work is a] marvel ~~of *Maldoror* is in its dialectical~~ [as a result of the] fusion of [t]his primary approach~~,~~ [and] this forethought, with ~~the~~ unsuspected [dream] insights ~~of oneirism~~, which [in it] were left to develop ~~within him~~ as freely as possible. ~~Compared to Lautréamont's great dialectical synthesis of consciously intended frames of mind with elements of the unconscious, many works of Surrealism, even Rimbaud's Illuminations, appear to be merely impressive — and this is because both Illuminations and Surrealist poetry to a large extent lack that one facet that is, as we can see, indispensable for greatness : conscious direction.~~

[ENTIRE PARAGRAPH EXPUNGED]

~~Lautréamont is such a marvelous example also because he lights our way today more than at any other time. No other~~

~~society will have such an ardent and tangible appreciation for the aspirations he demonstrated in *Poésies* as one that is built on hope and good, a socialist society.~~ If Lautréamont was wholly justified in rebuking the poseurs among the greatest poets of the past and of his era, while at the same time he inimitably towered over their faculties of imagination in terms of the power of ~~oneirism~~ [the dream], then more than anyone else ~~it is in his footsteps, as revealed as well as occluded by Surrealists, that~~ [we are called to follow in his revealed as well as obscured footsteps] to seek out a great ~~dialectical~~ synthesis of good in the service of life and the repressed malice of dream, between the benefits of a conscious poetic approach and the benefits of the incalculable potential of oneirism.

[8 ENTIRE PARAGRAPHS EXPUNGED]

Mood lighter, I return to the winding stairs down which Prague leads me. For as the daily droning of the bombers flying overhead has made clear, there is no time, time flies by and tomorrow might be too late. Our covenant with life is not forever, and your last testament cannot be put off indefinitely when confronted daily with the growing urgency to say everything, to say it all in a single sentence, to say more than ever needed to be said at any other time, to ask your steps with increasing anxiety where they are taking you, where they would like to take you, where they would rather not go at the cost of life, at the cost of death.

The poet is someone who destroys and creates myths, who destroys them to create new ones, always more real.

~~And a great new realism, its path having been cleared by Surrealism, is coming — it is on the way, it is being born.~~

[3 SECTIONS ADDED TO FILL OUT THE PAGES]

The Vltava sings its wordless song
The Vltava sings I give it the lyrics
Night spreads its net and the fishing begun
more radiant than an Allah panegyric
As the stars expired one after the other
in the pantomime of pale fish so sad without sound
like a wordless song like the roar of ancient wood

Come sweet Madelon come Hedvik come Kazi
Vltava sings while Madelon stays hazy

The Vltava surges over its banked verge
Night casts a veil over drowned women
whom I uncover like a prolonged dirge
a black requiem wreathed in whitened spume
As the women expired one after the other
in the pantomime of pale fish in the arms of black kings
like a wordless song like the roar of carnivaling

Come sweet Tereza Marie Ninon Kazi
Vltava sings while Madelon stays hazy

The Vltava glitters with festival mummery
Brass bands drumming I know not what to wail
Night spreads its net under black periphery
as the dead moon watched in a nun's veil
and the stars expired one after the other
in a pantomime of sparkler like the gleam of pearl

like a wordless song like the roar of long years
like sweet Tereza Marie Ninon Kazi

Vltava sings while Madelon stays hazy

Starstudded Vltava calmly winding through your nocturnal channel between two dissimilar halves of a torn black rose held together by the stitching of sturdy bridges, your darkening blood surges through the ancient wound of Prague's time-tested spell, all that pours into you, and yet right before our eyes you still fulfill your destiny : grandeur.

You are like a poet, Vltava, like one you have wellsprings in the childhood leas covered with the leaves and stalks of haymaking, and a frog sings by your spring, you are like a poet, Vltava. Like one having rushed into the world barefooted, indulging carefree in your intimate experiences and the soft nostrils of mares whose knees your badgering barely reaches, you are like a poet, Vltava. Like one you fly into the wide world without thought of your future meanders, through which rugged cliffs mercilessly buffet you, like one you chased your desire without ruler and compass, you are like a poet, Vltava. You are like a poet, Vltava, and like one you fondle rigid impediments to give them an amatory suppleness, you are like a poet, Vltava. You likewise drink in affluents, no matter whence they found their way to you, nor do you cap your avidity for the benefit of foreign wisdom, you are like a poet, Vltava. You carry off dog carcasses and rotted bottomless baskets and take into yourself the filth of humanity, you are like a poet, Vltava. A pig afflicted with ringworm which would kill even the hardiest bulldog finds in you its royal lye that will restore it to the health of nature, you are like a poet, Vltava. What of it if during spring rains you spill over your banks and drunkenly cling to trees and yank the hair thatches of innocent cottages, you are like a poet, Vltava. You have as well lascivious arms to embrace women bathing naked in the moonlight, you are like a poet, Vltava. You are forever rippled with a thousand memories and yet rarely turn back, you are like a poet. You, too, are not afraid of foreign influences and of drowning in a sea of nothingness or universality until your singular destiny has been fulfilled, you are like a poet, Vltava.

You are like a poet, Vltava. You flow under footbridges on which romp a dog, cat, and child, you are like a poet. You like to wet your lips and brow, to flow around wheels milling rye and wheat as you inalienably and eternally hurtle toward freedom like a poet, Vltava. Your waters are fed from the purest springs purling from the heavens and the worst filth from carrion dumps, you are like a poet. You drink barrels bursting in breweries, ferment causing flatulence and phlegm hocked into your subterranean springs, you are like a poet, Vltava. You give life to flowers and take people's breath away, you know how to caress with boundless gentleness but also how to freeze over and sink into solitude, you are like a poet, Vltava. You are older than Vyšehrad, a monument to your glory, old and new with each second, you are like a poet, Vltava. Like one you allow anyone whom it pleases to bend over a rod and fish from your inexhaustible treasures only to excoriate you, you are like a poet, Vltava. Like one you recycle human excrement and cleanse the most disgusting foulness, you are like a poet. You are like a poet. You allow those with measuring instruments to adapt you for their needs and the needs of humanity, and with the next step already unbounded like a poet. You accept all those who ply you with heavy loads or on a boat trip and do not protest against the jabs of ship pistons, you are like a poet, Vltava. You reflect the blue empyrean of spring, lightning storms, the obstinacy of morose skies, and the starry firmament, you are like a poet.

You could not bypass Prague, Vltava, nor her riverside taverns, nor her sewers that so insidiously flow into you as if meant to suffocate you, nor her predestined royal crown, Hradčany, you are like a poet, Vltava. Like one you have brought a complicated past to the capital city, like one, you have arrived blind to mirror the centuries-old beauty, like one you undermine the most majestic structures to rebuild them as ever more fanciful architecture, you are like a poet, Vltava. Like one, looked down on by dismissive glares, like one accepting lacing of regular and irregular stanzas, like one running to newer and newer horizons, you remain true to your Prague, you are like a poet, Vltava.

You are ineffable, Vltava, and it was the greatest musical genius of your people who cast a spell on you to bring you close to our hearts, a genius who went deaf from hearing the higher harmonies of springtimes, from resurrecting memories buried so deep they were nearly mute, having, like you, mastered with thousands of swirling fingers the pulsation of universal beauty, and like you, deeply sunk in native meadows, you are like a Czech poet, Vltava.

Starstudded Vltava, with you the most innocent creature wagers life and death, vulnerable and obliged to remind the poet that grandeur is his ultimate destiny, but you refused that sacrifice, and the poet also knows what it means to awaken Snow White from the dead with a kiss, his blood from your blood, Vltava, washes off and heals all wounds, Vltava, starstudded river flowing through Prague, impose your grandeur on us, Vltava, starstudded river.

On Golden Lane at Hradčany
time hardly even slips away
If you want to live five centuries
leave all behind for alchemy

When that simple miracle happens
the gold of our rivers will disappear
Farewell farewell you charlatans
Give our regards to the coming years

pp. 149-152

At another time, as I was crossing from Kaprova Street to that same little square (I don't know why I feel pulled there so often, to that very place where centuries earlier the people to whom Prague belongs seemed as if they would be subjugated forever), I imagined I was living in an age in which the astrological calendar nearly always indicated auspicious configurations, that the era of impending wars had already passed, ~~that the era of hunger, unfreedom, the lawful destruction of one human being by another had already passed,~~ that justice had already prevailed, that ~~the seed sown in the blood of the East twenty years ago~~ [it] had already yielded its radiant fruits. I imagined myself sauntering through Prague ~~in a time when~~

~~human prehistory had arrived,~~ in a time when the right to act and the right to dream were dispensed more fairly — and I relished the fact that Prague~~, imprecations flying over her flagstones, as they must,~~ had remained true to herself, more than at any other time had remained true to herself! I saw her arcane beauty reincarnated in the people who will be born in a happier age for humanity than the era that has chosen us as the prime movers of time and revolutionary history. I thought of you who are still to come. I thought of you in Prague. I thought of you and your earnest or jubilant voices, which embody something of the voices of those ~~marching~~ youth who today have occupied all of Prague's sidewalks, crowding out all the traffic from her streets, rendering it utterly fatuous in these youthful faces, in the faces of those with aspirations higher than ours, that they will see how a justice much greater than we have known goes hand in hand with Prague's beauty.

~~Before I set down the pen, I would like to yield to the spark I felt blazing up in my spirit as I stood before that bridge in Leningrad spanning the Neva as an extension of the former Nevsky Prospekt, standing several steps away from the Winter Palace with a view of the Peter and Paul Fortress and the lighthouse, whose light mill would start up as soon as evening fell, when I suddenly had the sensation that my mind, so attentive to the delights of analogy, had migrated to that part of Prague near the Parliament at the end of Mánes Bridge with its vista of Hradčany, Letná Hill, and the broad swath of the Vltava hidden under her bridges.~~

At that moment, ~~when the beauty of Leningrad and of Prague unexpectedly and solemnly clasped hands in my imagination,~~ I fell in love with Prague in all her splendor, looking forward to the future. And in my mind then, ~~my eyes fixed on dazzling white sailors kissing their girlfriends over the Neva as night fell,~~ I gave an innocent kiss as well to You, ~~whom I didn't yet know,~~ I kissed You as my desire. Patience, please! Isn't the hope of such a kiss, now almost completely divorced from all practical necessity, enough for us to spurn all the justified hideousness of anxiety, each onset of irony and cynicism that tries to steal onto the edge of our lips? And if we are not destined to personally taste the beneficence of such a kiss, isn't the mere hope of it enough for us to experience everything that is happening around us today, everything weighing on us, everything we would like to banish from our lives, like the middle act of a drama that ends with the singing of an ode to joy? I have not forgotten the kiss ~~of those sailors and Leningrad girls~~. I have not forgotten the light I saw blaze like a celebratory rocket over Prague ~~when it appeared to me on~~ that bridge ~~in Leningrad~~. I have not forgotten it today, particularly today, when it's become imperative to draw on everything that could offer hope, when it's become imperative to array all glimmers of hope against any thought of hopelessness and despair ~~arising from the awareness that tomorrow or the day after we might have to part with life~~. Yet over and above this very awareness, the awareness that ~~we~~ [all of us] might be called to [the most bitter] duty, called to enter her service, I realize, as her clock towers chime one-thirty, that Prague is eternal, realize how Prague is eternal.

And her eternalness, which I do not doubt even when confronted with ~~a~~ [the most chilling] vision ~~of her roofs engulfed in flame~~, bears traces of us, will bear traces of us. Do not be afraid to utter this last sentence, errant soul!

Tomorrow a swallow will carry this sentence to the window you have thus far neglected to look at. This sentence will not be lost in either time or space, even though it will leave no vestige of itself. It will become something as moving and negligible as one of the small stones on ~~Rabbi Loew's~~ [a] tomb. But it will not be lost. And if at one time birds wake up people and at another time people wake up birds, it's all good. It is also worth noting that black stones layered on top of one another centuries ago can sometimes stir the human heart. Who knows what would have befallen my brothers, those with whom I share a common language and a common fate, if it were not for Prague, if those who lived long before us had not succeeded in creating this talisman. This talisman, which has the power to mesmerize our eyes with dream, this talisman, for whose preservation we are willing and determined to take whatever action whenever necessary.

NOTES

11 The Absolute Gravedigger: *Absolutní hrobař*, published in 1937 by František Borový in Prague, English translation by Stephan Delbos and Tereza Novická published in 2016 by Twisted Spoon Press in Prague. Just as *The Absolute Gravedigger* completed a Surrealist triptych that included *Woman in the Plural* and *Prague with Fingers of Rain*, *A Prague Flâneur* completed in parallel an autobiographical prose triptych, influenced by André Breton's *Nadja*, that also comprised *Invisible Moscow* and *Rue Gît-le-Coeur* (see below).

11 *Smíchov:* a sprawling district on the left bank of the Vltava adjacent to Malá Strana (Lesser Town).

11 *Kinský Garden:* Kinského zahrada, a park at the base of Petřín Hill at the boundary dividing Smíchov from Malá Strana. The Kinský Summer Palace at one end has been part of the National Museum since 1922 and houses the ethnographic exhibition.

11 *Jiří Wolker:* (1900–24) Czech poet, journalist, and playwright, one of the founding members of the Communist Party of Czechoslovakia, a leading proponent of "proletarian" poetry and closely involved with the avant-garde artists' group Devětsil.

12 *Jakub Deml:* (1878–1961), Moravian priest, poet, and writer, associated with early 20th-century Expressionism and Catholic Modernism. Nezval was a close friend.

13 *eight Soviet generals:* As part of Stalin's Great Purge, Marshal Mikhail Tukhachevsky and seven other high-ranking Red Army officers were charged with espionage in connection with a "Trotskyist" plot, the evidence of which had been fabricated. The trial was secret, the confessions coerced, and all eight summarily executed on June 11-12, 1937.

14 *Demyan Bedny:* the pen name of Yefim Alekseevich Pridvorov (1883–1945), poet, Bolshevik propagandist, stalwart supporter and personal friend of Vladimir Lenin, awarded the Order of Lenin in 1933.

14 *"But this is not the studied, . . .":* The quote comes from Nikolai Bukharin, "Poetry, Poetics and the Problems of Poetry in the U.S.S.R." (delivered in 1934), the English translation comes from *Gorky, Radek, Bukharin, Zhdanov and others "Soviet Writers' Congress 1934"* (London: Martin Lawrence Ltd., 1935), 185-258.

14 *RAPP:* Rossiyskaya Assotsiatsiya Proletarskikh Pisateley [Russian Association of Proletarian Writers] took its name in 1928 and was the precursor of the Union of Soviet Writers that was formed in 1932.

15 *the Stalin Constitution:* The Soviet Constitution of 1936, also known as the "Stalin Constitution," remained in force until 1977.

15 The Breasts of Tiresias: *Les mamelles de Tirésias*, Apollinaire's play from 1903, whose 1917 production included the subtitle: "A Surrealist Drama," thus coining the word "surrealism."

16 *Café Hlavova:* Hlavova kavárna occupied the entire ground floor of No. 1219 at náměstí Míru in Prague 2 and was the culture and social center of the Vinohrady district. It no longer exists.

16 *Hanau Pavilion:* Hanavský pavilon sits atop the hill at the edge of Letná Park overlooking the Vltava. Neo-Baroque and built in 1891, it was donated to Prague by the Prince of Hanau.

16 *Žofín Palace:* Palác Žofín is a Neo-Renaissance building dating to 1885 on Slovanský ostrov (Slavonic Island). A traditional venue for balls and concerts.

16 *Municipal Commons:* Měšťanská beseda, 21 Vladislavova Street, Prague's New Town, built in 1871 in classicist style and serving as the meeting place for a number of associations and societies. It is now a hotel.

16 *Municipal House:* Obecní dům, grand Art-Nouveau building in Prague 1 constructed during the first decade of the 20th century, containing a popular café, restaurants, a concert hall, and exhibition spaces.

16 *poetry for all five senses:* Cf. Karel Teige's "Manifesto of Poetism" from 1928 in which he proposes a poetry for the five senses.

16 Život: "Life," a review of literature and art published from 1921 to 1948, and relaunched in 2005.

16 *the small Na Slupi theater:* performance space for both amateur and professional theater in operation 1925–64 and situated in a building on Na Slupi Street in Prague 2 that was demolished in 1975.

16 *Jarmila Horákova:* (1904–28), talented stage actress, who during her short life appeared in 85 roles in over 300 performances, including the first Liberated Theater in 1926, as well as in several films.

16 Dispatch on Wheels: Nezval's avant-garde play *Depeše na kolečkách* written in 1922 as a text and first staged by Liberated Theater in 1926. It was included in the collection *Pantomima* (1924).

17 *Josef Čapek:* (1887–1945), painter, graphic artist, book illustrator, author, brother of Karel Čapek.

17 The Gimpy Pilgrim: *Kulhavý poutník,* a book of essays by Josef Čapek published in 1936.

17 The Heresiarch & Co.: *L'Hérèsiarque et Cie,* Guillaume Apollinaire's first book, a collection of stories published in 1910 that includes "Le passant de Prague" (known in English translation as "The Wandering Jew").

17 *Legion Bridge:* Most Legií, the National Theater is located at one end, the edge of Malá Strana at the other.

17 *Na Příkopě:* (lit. "on the moat") in Prague 1, begins at the bottom of Wenceslas Square near the end of Národní třída (National Avenue), picking up on the other side as a pedestrian upscale shopping area. Among Prague Germans it was known as the Graben.

17 *at each stop:* At that time a tram line ran along the bottom and the length of Wenceslas Square.

22 *Mánes:* functionalist building erected in 1930 on a branch of the Vltava next to Slavonic Island as the seat of the Association of Fine Artists Mánes, including an exhibition space, restaurant, and café terrace.

22 *All-Union Congress of Soviet Writers:* First held in August 1934, it ushered in Socialist Realism as the prevailing artistic dogma.

22 *tower of the former mill:* Mánes was built on the site of the old Šítkovské mills, which were demolished to clear space, yet preserving the 15th-century water tower, which is still standing.

22 *Hřebenka:* an area of Smíchov southwest of Petřin Hill.

25 *Hynek Bookshop:* Alois Hynek established a publishing house and bookstore in 1869 at 11 Celetná Street. It remained family-owned and in operation until it was nationalized in 1949.

27 *Antonín Slavíček:* (1870–1910), Czech Impressionist painter.

28 *Rubeš Gallery:* At this location from 1916 to 1938, now the Václav Špála Gallery (Galerie Václava Špály).

30 *Petřín Terrace:* Restaurace Petřínské terasy, an expansive veranda that overlooks Prague from the slope of Petřín Hill, is still in operation.

31 *Jirásek Bridge:* Jiráskův most, was built to connect Jirásek Square in New Town with the Dientzenhofer Gardens in Smíchov.

34 *Seminary Garden:* Seminářská zahrada, located on the eastern slope of Petřín Hill, a public park since 1930 with numerous fruit trees, formerly the gardens of the Carmelite Convent.

34 *Pohořelec:* formerly a settlement, an open area on the western edge of Prague Castle adjacent to the Strahov Monastery, dominated by the former Hradčany Barracks complex.

37 *town of the deranged:* the Bohnice psychiatric hospital complex, dominated by a water tower, is over the hill from Troja.

37 *Kobylisy:* a suburb of Prague, just to the east of Troja and Bohnice.

38 *Stromovka:* large tree park in Prague 7 just across the river from Troja.

38 *Josef Kolínský:* (1897–1923) was executed for the robbery and murder of watchmaker and goldsmith Josef Ledecky and his wife and daughter, a crime he committed with his brother, Jan, after both had been recently made unemployed. Josef was wounded three times in WWI and decorated for bravery. President T.G. Masaryk commuted Jan's death sentence to life in prison, but refused Josef's request. On the morning of his execution, Josef's final words were: "Mr. President, my final words are that I wish you a long and healthy reign."

39 Mayor Dietrich: Baron Philippe Friedrich Dietrich (1748–93) was the first mayor of Strasbourg.

39 *Zbraslav:* originally an independent municipality on the Vltava's left bank, incorporated into Prague in 1974 as the city's southernmost district.

39 *"Chimera":* a poem in Nezval's collection *Hra v kostky: básně 1927 a 1928* [A Game of Dice: Poetry 1927 and 1928] (Prague: R. Škeřík, 1928), in which he says farewell to his romantic lyric.

39 *Hotel Bavaria:* a somewhat seedy hotel with a café and tavern that was located at 42 Na Poříčí Street next to Hotel Axa. Generally thought to be where Apollinaire stayed during his celebrated visit to Prague in 1902, the building was demolished in the 1930s.

40 *Konstantin Biebl:* (1898–1951) poet and occasional prose writer, member of the avant-garde group Devětsil and an original member of the Surrealist Group in Czechoslovakia, initially stood with Nezval in the pro-Moscow camp.

40 *U Leflérů:* a late-night "café" frequented by newspapermen and such literati as Jakub Arbes and Jiří Karásek ze Lvovic, usually ending up there after the pubs closed.

40 *Malostranská Café:* Malostranská kavárna, located on Malostranské Square, was a famous haunt of artists and writers through the 1990s. It is now a Starbucks.

40 *the Pigeons:* U Holubů at 7 Štefánikova Street, Smíchov. A classic pub that in the early 1990s also served as gambling den, nightclub, brothel, and noted meeting place for the Russian mob. It closed soon after a police raid in 1995.

40 *Karlín:* a Prague district straddling the right bank of the Vltava south of the city center.

40 *Košíře:* Part of the Smíchov district, the neighborhood was once a village in the 19th century, then an independent town before being incorporated into Greater Prague in 1922, becoming a working-class suburb that provided housing for the labor of Smíchov's factories.

41 *Parliament:* from 1919 to 1939 located in the Rudolfinum.

43 *Old Demínka:* The Demínka restaurant and café was established in 1886 and is located to this day on the corner of Škrétova Street in Prague 2. In Nezval's day it was commonly referred to as Stará [Old] Demínka.

44 *overthrow of the government:* Upon hearing that Austria-Hungary had accepted the armistice conditions that would end WWI, the National Council in Prague declared Czechoslovakia an independent state on

October 28, 1918, and seized the reigns of power in what was, essentially, a peaceful coup.

44 *the Tůmovka:* Café Tůmova was established in 1872 at 4 Lazarská Street in Prague's New Town. A celebrated literary café, it was the favorite haunt of Jaroslav Hašek, who wrote many of his "humoresques" here. In the 1950s it was transferred to the administration of the state restaurant enterprise and converted into a workers canteen, which continued in operation until the 1990s.

44 *the Unionka:* Café Union was located on the corner of Na Perštýně and Národní třída and known as an artists café. Surviving into the 1940s, the building was demolished in 1949-50 and the new building served as the headquarters for the children's publisher Albatros into the 1990s. It is now a bank.

44 *V.H. Bruner* [sic]: Vratislav Hugo Brunner (1886–1928), typographer, illustrator, graphic artist, caricaturist, and designer of games and stage sets.

44 *Jindřich Hořejší:* (1886–1941), poet, translator, member of Devětsil. Having studied at the Sorbonne, he translated Hašek's *The Good Soldier Švejk* into French.

45 *Café Slovanka:* Located at 17 Na Moráni Street in Prague's New Town, it no longer exists, but another café occupies the space.

45 *Jiří Mahen:* born Antonín Vančura (1882–1939), poet, journalist, playwright, theater director and critic, a cousin of Vladislav Vančura.

46 *Jan Mukařovský:* (1891–1975), the leading Czech linguist and aesthetic theorist of his era, associated with structuralism and the Prague Linguistic Circle.

48 *St. Thomas Brewery:* The brewery was established in the Augustine monastery of St. Thomas in Malá Strana in 1352 and brewed its own dark beer until 1952. During the early 20th century its cellar tavern was frequented by many artists. It is now a luxury hotel with upscale restaurant and pub.

50 *elections a few years back:* In the Czechoslovak parliamentary elections of 1935 the Sudeten German Party, newly created and led by Konrad Henlein, received the most votes to the Chamber of Deputies and to the Senate (15% in both cases).

50 *Ignát Herrmann:* (1854–1935) humorist and writer of stories, novels, and feuilletons that provided idyllic motifs for many popular Czech films of the 1930s.

52 Made in . . . : as it appears in English in the original; the three members of the Axis.

52 *with braided whip:* A reference to the Czech Easter folk custom whereby boys with whips of braided willow twigs and decorated with ribbons chase girls who are "gently" whipped when caught.

53 Invisible Moscow: *Neviditelná Moskva* (Prague: František Borovy, 1935), Nezval's lyrical account of his stay in Moscow in the summer of 1934 soon after the founding of the Surrealist Group in Czechoslovakia.

53 Rue Gît-le-Coeur: *Ulice Gît-le-coeur* (Prague: František Borovy, 1936), recounts Nezval's 1935 stay in Paris to attend the First International Congress of Writers.

53 *one of those nightspots on National Avenue:* The meeting took place at the wine bar U Locha at 7 Národní třída, which eventually became the Poetic Wine Bar Viola in 1963 and is today's Theater Viola.

54 *the Radek Trial:* Karl Radek (1885–1939), a close collaborator with Lenin and former Secretary of the Comintern, ultimately confessed to treason at the Trial of the Seventeen in 1937. Sentenced to ten years in the gulag, he was killed in 1939.

55 *his run-in with Ehrenburg:* In June 1935, the First International Congress of Writers for the Defense of Culture was held in Paris at Maison de la Mutualité. Just weeks before Breton had confronted Ilya Ehrenburg on the street and repeatedly slapped him, the infamous incident witnessed by Nezval. Ehrenburg, who was on the organizing committee for the Congress, took his revenge by having Breton removed from the program.

56 *the Toyen and Štyrský exhibition:* Nezval wrote the Introduction and included a poem dedicated to the artists in the monograph *Štyrský a Toyen*, afterword by Karel Teige (Prague: František Borovy, 1938).

57 Haló News: *Haló noviny*, between 1933–38 a Leftist oriented newspaper largely echoing the official line of the Czechoslovak Communist Party, was revived in 1991 as the daily newspaper of the Communist

Party of Bohemia and Moravia before transitioning into a weekly magazine under a different name in 2022.

59 *their pamphlet:* This would be *Surrealismus proti proudu* [Surrealism against the Current], penned by Karel Teige and published in 1938 by the Surrealist Group in Prague. It bore the subtitle: "The Surrealist Group answers Vítězslav Nezval, J. Fučík, Kurt Konrad, St. K. Neumann, J. Rybák, L. Štoll, et al."

61 *guided my steps:* In May 1933, Nezval, visiting Paris for the first time, had a chance encounter with Breton in Café de la place Blanche, deciding soon after to found the Surrealist Group in Czechoslovakia.

63 *and appear nevermore:* Nezval translated E. A. Poe's "The Raven" into Czech, and the reference here is no doubt deliberate.

64 *Machar:* Josef Svatopluk Machar (1864–1942), bureaucrat, poet, prose writer, columnist, and politician, coauthor of the "Manifesto of Czech Modernism" (1895) and a proponent of Critical Realism.

64 *Sova:* Antonín Sova, (1864–1928), poet, writer influenced by Symbolism and Impressionism, and first director of the Prague Municipal Library.

64 *Fráňa Šrámek:* (1877–1952), poet, writer, playwright, anarchist firebrand. The antiwar poetry collection *Splav* [The Weir] was published in 1916 and an expanded edition (with war poetry) in 1922; the novel *Tělo* [Body] was published in 1919.

64 *Štefánik Barracks:* Štefánikova kasarna, built in 1892 and located at Kinský Square in Prague's Smíchov district, was converted in the 1990s into the seat of the municipal court (Palace of Justice).

66 *Gustav Pfleger Moravský:* (1833–75), Moravian poet, novelist, and playwright.

66 *Karel Hlaváček:* (1874–98), Prague poet and artist, one of the leading representatives of Czech Decadence and Symbolism, who was born and died in the working-class district of Libeň.

67 Edison: Comprising five cantos and written in 1927, the poetic counterpart to Karel Teige's "Manifesto of Poetism," it was published in Prague as a separate volume in 1928 by Rudolf Škeřík in Edition Plejada.

67 *Mírové Square:* Mírové náměstí (Peace Square) from 1927 to 1948, originally Purkyňovo náměstí (mentioned below) when established in 1884 and renamed in 1948 to its present náměstí Míru.

68 Acrobat: *Akrobat* (Prague: Edition Plejada, Rudolf Škeřík, 1928) proto-Surrealist free verse comprising three cantos and influenced by Apollinaire's "Zone" that had appeared in Czech thanks to Karel Čapek's translation.

70 *Bedřich Vaníček:* (1885–1955), painter and translator who divided his time between Třebíč and Prague. He co-translated with Nezval the work of French Surrealists.

70 *Král Jiří Square:* Náměstí krále Jiřího (King George Square) the center of the Vinohrady neighborhood, was established in 1896 and renamed in 1948 to its current náměstí Jiřího z Poděbrad.

84 *A man or a stone . . . :* Translated by Alexis Lykiard in *Maldoror & the Complete Works of Comte de Lautréamont* (Cambridge: Exact Change, 1994).

86 *Wilson Station:* Prague's main train station, opened in 1871 as Emperor Franz Joseph Station until 1919, when it was renamed in honor of Woodrow Wilson. It has been called simply Main Station since 1953.

88 *Karlovy lázně:* a Gothic bathhouse right next to the Old Town Bridge Tower dating to the late 14th century, now a multistory nightclub.

90 *Josefovská Street:* Josefovská ulice in Josefov, the Jewish Quarter, was renamed in 1958 to today's Široká ulice.

94 *the square on U Radnice Street:* known during Nezval's life as Mikulášské náměstí (Nicholas Square), as it abuts the Church of St. Nicholas, it was renamed in 2000 for Franz Kafka (Náměstí Franze Kafky) and is where he was born in 1883.

94 *Iron Knight:* sometimes referred to as the Iron Man, is a monument created by the sculptor Ladislav Šaloun to the tragic legend of Jáchym Berka, a medieval knight who murdered his betrothed in a fit of jealous rage and was cursed by her to turn to stone. He can only be freed once every one hundred years by the kiss of a virgin with a pure heart. Apparently his next chance comes in 2109.

95 *Jan Mydlář:* (1572–1664), the most famous executioner in Czech history and the patriarch of a dynasty of executioners. It was he who in June 1621 on Old Town Square beheaded the 27 leaders of the Bohemian Estates Uprising, going through four swords to complete the job.

95 *monument to Ernest Denis:* For his role in the establishment of Czechoslovakia as an independent state, the Denis monument was unveiled on Malostranské Square in 1928. It was eventually demolished by Nazi authorities in 1941.

97 *St. Stephen's Church:* The Gothic kostel sv. Štěpána was established along with New Town by Charles IV in the mid-14th century.

97 *Emmaus Monastery:* Known as Na Slovanech from the Middle Ages, a Benedictine abbey of the Slavic Order established in 1347 by Charles IV; it suffered extensive bomb damage during WWII.

102 *After we had signed the guest book . . . :* these two paragraphs are taken nearly verbatim from Vítězslav Nezval, *Woman in the Plural*, trans. by Stephan Delbos and Tereza Novická (Prague: Twisted Spoon Press, 2021), 56-57.

103 *"Ragman":* "Hadrář" in *Hra v kostky* [A Game of Dice] (1928).

114 *cemetery at Vyšehrad:* the final resting place for many of the luminaries of Czech culture, including Antonín Dvořák, Bedřich Smetana, K.H. Mácha, Alfons Mucha, Božena Němcová, Karel Čapek, and, ultimately, Vítězslav Nezval himself.

115 *National Café:* Národní kavárna, opened in 1922 at 11 Národní třída, the main haunt of the Devětsil artists and the scene of a major brouhaha among them in 1929. Closed in 1948 to become a gallery of glass and decorative art, it was revived as a café in 2007.

122 *Technical Museum:* Originally housed in Schwarzenberg Palace (thus the reference), the museum moved to its present building next to Letná Park in 1942 and is now called the National Technical Museum.

124 *the bar U Černošek:* lit. At the Black Ladies, the "bar's" exact location is unclear, and it might be nothing more than mental association.

124 *Grégrova Street:* renamed to today's Slavíkova Street in 1961.

125 *food border:* In 1829, the Austrian Empire instituted an excise tax on foodstuffs and certain other goods coming into cities from the surrounding areas. It was known as the "food line" and applied to some of the larger cities such as Brno, Prague, Kraków, Lvov, Vienna, and Linz. Excise houses were built around the perimeter of Prague at important access roads to enforce the collection of duties and also serve as housing for family members of the "financial guard." Some of these buildings have been demolished and some have survived and been renovated. The tax was renewed by independent Czechoslovakia in 1921 and remained in force until 1942.

129 *Strasburk Tavern:* located in the Bohnice district and dating to the early 19th century, renovated and repurposed as a hospice at the beginning of the 20th century, which function it serves today.

130 *ČKD factory:* Českomoravská Kolben-Daněk was formed from a 1927 merger of two companies founded in the 19th century to become one of the country's largest engineering concerns, producing trams, locomotives, motorcycles, and, later, tanks.

130 *the Spider:* U Pavouka on Celetná Street in Old Town, a notorious tavern that features prominently in Paul Leppin's novella *Severin's Journey into the Dark.*

131 *U Rozvařilů:* Originally a brewpub located at 26 Na Poříčí with a nightclub (cabaret) in the courtyard since 1907, the brewery ceased operation in 1922 and the pub and cabaret in 1936 when the building was torn down. In 1937-38 Legiobanka built on the site, which was next door, a modern functionalist building with passageway, and U Rozvařilů reopened as a popular café and restaurant in the back through the passageway, and cafeteria facing the street. It closed in 2009, relocating to across the street, and the original space facing the street is now occupied by a Starbucks.

132 *Karlín Variety Theater:* founded in the 1870s and serving as a variety theater until 1939, since 1945 the Music Theater of Karlín.

136 *Karlova Street:* the former Karlova ulice in Žižkov, today's Seifertova ulice.

136 *Fochova Avenue:* Fochova třída from 1922 until 1940, named for

Marshal Ferdinand Foch, Supreme Allied Commander during WWI, taking its current name of Vinohradská třída in 1962.

137 *Maršner chocolate factory:* František Maršner and his wife Albina established a confectioner business in 1891 to make Turkish delight, and in 1896 they built a factory for chocolate and other confections on Korunní třída in the Vinohrady district, next to the brewery. In 1914, it launched the famous Orion brand of chocolates, the company eventually taking that for its name (now owned by Nestlé). The Vinohrady factory shut down in 1952.

139 *Podskalské Embankment:* Podskalské nábřeží, today's Rašínovo nábřeží.

141 *Bertramka:* A classical-style villa and former vineyard in the Košíře neighborhood of Smíchov dating to the early 18th century, it is famous for housing Mozart and where he worked on his opera *Don Giovanni*, which premiered in October 1787 at Prague's Estates Theater. Today the building and grounds are a museum to Mozart's stay and quiet little park close by the district's busiest streets.

142 *May 20, 1938:* the so-called May Crisis. After annexing Austria in March 1938, Nazi Germany continued to stir up unrest in Czechoslovakia's Sudeten regions. On May 19, reports came of a build-up of German forces on the border, appearing to indicate an imminent attack. Czechoslovakia responded on May 20 with the mobilization of army reserves. By May 23, in the absence of any actual military activity (and after British and French warnings to Germany), the immediate crisis had passed.

161 *Márinka:* a short text by Karel Hynek Mácha in which he tells of walking on an isolated path and encountering a beggar with a violin who handed him a piece of paper with the address of his daughter, who was very ill and was a great admirer of Mácha's poetry. He pays the sick girl a visit and is astounded not only by how beautifully she plays piano and sings, but her physical beauty, too, especially in contrast to the squalor of her life. He visits her once more and promises to come again when he returns from a journey. Upon his return, he learns that she has died and her father, grief-stricken, has drowned himself.

161 *Kanálka Garden:* Zahrada Kanálka, abolished in 1884 to make way for building projects, occupied the space of today's Polska Street,

Vinohrady Avenue, and part of the hillside park Riegrovy sady (Rieger Gardens).

162 *Jakub Arbes:* (1840–1914), native of the Smíchov district, Czech novelist who created the "romanetto" genre and was an admirer and translator of Edgar Allan Poe's work.

162 *Jaroslav Vrchlický:* (1853–1912), lyrical poet, writer, playwright, and translator, nominated eight times for the Nobel Prize in Literature.

174 The Mysteries of Prague: *Tajnosti pražské*, inspired by Eugène Sue's *Les Mystères de Paris*, a historical novel written in 1868 by Josef Svátek (1835–97) and republished in many editions over the first decades of the 20th century.

175 *Kondelík:* The two novels *Otec Kondelík a ženich Vejvara* [1898; Papa Kondelík and Bridegroom Vejvara] and its sequel *Tchán Kondelík a zeť Vejvara* [1906; Father-in-law Kondelík and Son-in-law Vejvara] by Ignát Herrmann (see note above) were humorous portraits of Prague family life.

VÍTĚZSLAV NEZVAL (1900–58) was perhaps the leading Czech avant-garde writer of the entire 20th century. A founding member of both Devětsil in 1920 and the Surrealist Group in Czechoslovakia in 1934 (the first such group outside of France), Nezval's oeuvre consists of numerous poetry collections, experimental plays and novels, memoirs, essays, and translations. In addition to *The Absolute Gravedigger*, his most important work includes *Pantomime*, *Prague with Fingers of Rain*, *Valerie and Her Week of Wonders*, and *A Prague Flâneur*. Along with Karel Teige, Jindřich Štyrský, and Toyen, Nezval forged ties with the French Surrealists. He served as editor of the Czech group's journal *Surrealismus*.

JED SLAST is a native of Richmond, Virginia, who lives in Prague. His translations from Czech include *Edition 69*, *Dreamverse* by Jindřich Štyrský, and *A Postmortem Dream* by Ladislav Klíma.

A PRAGUE FLÂNEUR

by Vítězslav Nezval

Translated by Jed Slast from the original
Czech *Pražský chodec* first published
in 1938 by František Borový in Prague

Cover and design by Silk Mountain

Cutout image of Charles Bridge from
original cover by František Muzika

Set in Garamond Pro / Univers

FIRST EDITION PUBLISHED IN 2024

Twisted Spoon Press
P.O. Box 21 — Preslova 12
150 00 Prague 5
Czech Republic
www.twistedspoon.com

Printed and bound in the Czech Republic
by TISKÁRNA PROTISK, České Budějovice

Trade distribution:

UK & Europe
CENTRAL BOOKS
www.centralbooks.com

US & Canada
SCB DISTRIBUTORS
www.scbdistributors.com